BITTER
ROOTS

BITTER ROOTS

JOHN L. MOORE

THOMAS NELSON PUBLISHERS
Nashville

Published in Nashville, Tennessee, by Thomas Nelson, Inc., and distributed in Canada by Lawson Falle, Ltd., Cambridge, Ontario.

Scripture quotations are from the NEW KING JAMES VERSION of the Bible. Copyright © 1979, 1980, 1982, Thomas Nelson, Inc., Publishers.

Library of Congress Cataloging-in-Publication Data

Moore, John L.
     Bitter roots ; a novel / by John L. Moore.
         p. cm.
     "A Jan Dennis book."
     ISBN 0-8407-6759-5 (pbk.)
     1. Family—United States—Fiction. I. Title.
PS3563.06214B5   1993
813'.54—dc20   93-24126
                                                   CIP

Printed in the United States of America
1 2 3 4 5 6 7 8 9   98 97 96 95 94 93

DEDICATION

This novel was originally titled "Ornery Men." It is dedicated to my sisters, Patricia and Debbie, and to my cousin Linda, because between them they have known their share of ornery men.

ACKNOWLEDGEMENTS

I would like to thank my editor, Jan Dennis, for always believing in this book; his former assistant, Jennifer Nahrstadt, for her opinions; my publisher, Bruce Barbour, for his support; and the following men for being models of spiritual masculinity: John Sanford, Post Falls, Idaho; Ras Robinson, Fort Worth, Texas; Charles Greene, Nashville, Tennessee; Charles Snell, Spray, Oregon; and Curt Thorne, Eldon Toews, Rod Lee, and Joe Peila, Miles City, Montana. And, I can't thank my wife, Debra, enough for being an example of a godly woman.

Pursue peace with all men, and holiness, without which no one will see the Lord: looking diligently lest anyone fall short of the grace of God; lest any root of bitterness springing up cause trouble, and by this many become defiled.

Hebrews 12:14-15

The McColley Family Tree

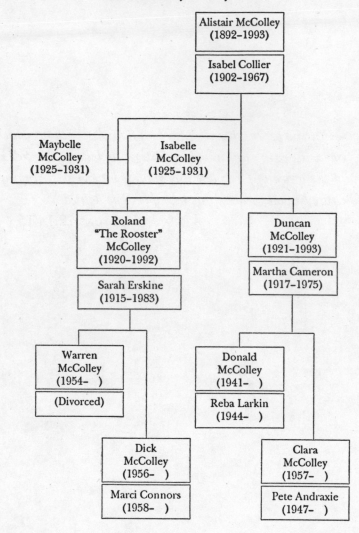

Alistair McColley
(1892–1993)

Isabel Collier
(1902–1967)

Maybelle
McColley
(1925–1931)

Isabelle
McColley
(1925–1931)

Roland
"The Rooster"
McColley
(1920–1992)

Sarah Erskine
(1915–1983)

Duncan
McColley
(1921–1993)

Martha Cameron
(1917–1975)

Warren
McColley
(1954–)

(Divorced)

Donald
McColley
(1941–)

Reba Larkin
(1944–)

Dick
McColley
(1956–)

Marci Connors
(1958–)

Clara
McColley
(1957–)

Pete Andraxie
(1947–)

1
The Reunion

This is a beautiful land, eastern Montana. A stark, handsome, masculine land. Long-limbed by prairie and muscled with rolling hills; wrinkled with badlands; tanned by a bald treelessness. It is not a nurturing land. It yields nothing willingly. It is a man's land, where men can turn their weathered faces into yet another storm and believe in tomorrow. Tough men. Ornery men.

The land suffers under the curse. From the ripening wheat fields glowing golden in the sun, to the brittle clay gumbo of the plains, weeds infest this land. Leafy spurge, knapweed, Canadian thistle. They, too, are tough, ornery—resilient. Clip them at the stem, and the roots spread in a self-preserving cultivation. Poison them and you poison yourself and all the plants about them. Their roots tap deep into the soil seeking and finding life in the earth's depths. They reproduce through flowers that dry into winged seeds riding the breezes like rumors thrown into the wind. To kill the plant, you must kill the root.

I love this land. I was born to it forty-nine years ago on a farm north of Great Falls. I was born again fourteen years later beneath the tent of an itinerant evangelist. When I was sixteen my parents were killed on a graveled country road. I stayed on the farm. Land is life here. Three years later, I met, and eventually married, Donald McColley.

It is a very unusual story I tell. It is the story of my husband's grandfather, Alistair Angus McColley, and his seed.

It is a spiritual story, not a mystical one. I am not a mystic. I am charismatic by experience, but the church I attend is not. I restrain myself for Donald's sake.

My story takes place at the Pioneer Museum in Yellow Rock, Montana, in April of the past year. The museum was honoring the late Alistair McColley by inducting him into their Pioneer Hall of Fame. For the first time in years, all of the McColley family were together. Even those considered missing.

Alistair Angus McColley was born in Scotland. He raised two sons, Roland and Duncan. Roland had one son, my Donald, and a daughter, Clara. Duncan had two sons, Warren and Dick.

Alistair became well-known as a sheepman. And as the man who killed the Big Swede. He was rumored to be a man of money, but no one has found it. He died this past January at the age of one hundred in a nursing home in Yellow Rock while his family searched the hills in a blizzard, not for missing gold, but for the body of his son, Duncan. My husband's father.

This could be a difficult, confusing story to tell if I tried to tell it myself. But I will tell it as it was told to me: each person speaking their innermost thoughts—secretly, unknowingly—into my innermost ear.

Yellow Rock is a little cowtown that sits alongside a lazy, muddy river. The museum is nestled in a cove of cotton-woods at the town's edge. Donald and I arrived early because he had been chosen to give the induction speech. He was very nervous. It was his task, he believed, not to merely eulogize his grandfather, but to immortalize a generation of pioneers and the bloodline of the McColley clan.

Donald's main concern was death and presumed death.

"What do I do about the Big Swede?" he asked me again, holding his bald head in his hands. Premature baldness is hereditary in the McColley family. When Donald strains to think, conduits of blue veins pulsate under his scalp like glowing electrical lines.

"I wouldn't mention it," I said. Guests were beginning to filter into the banquet hall. Most of them were elderly.

"What about my father? Do I say anything about old Duncan being missing? I mean, everyone knows—"

"It doesn't need to be mentioned," I replied.

"But both would add color," he said. "The killing of the Big Swede, my father lost in a blizzard, Grandpa's missing gold . . ."

"It sounds like a poem by Robert Service," I said, then I regretted bringing it up. Donald fancies himself a poet.

"A poem. A long epic poem. That's what I should have done. Why didn't I think of that?"

I saw Clara McColley enter the room. "Your sister is here," I said.

"A poem. I wonder if I have time . . ."

Clara entered stiffly as if braced against a wind. She is thirty-five, seventeen years younger than Donald. The age span has made them strangers. Clara will never have to worry about weight—she has the McColley leanness honed to a sharp edge and is quite capable of being pretty but seldom makes the attempt. She imagines herself as old, weathered, and ignorant and wants nothing from life but a home in the country with Pete Andraxie. He followed her in. Donald was bent over his notebook scribbling notes. "Pete Andraxie is here," I said.

"What's he doing here?" he snarled without looking up.

"He came with Clara."

"Hmmrrff. I should have known. Well, if Pa is dead this will be enough to rattle him out of his grave."

I placed a restraining hand on Donald's shoulder as I got up from my chair.

"Where you going?" he asked.

"I am going to greet Clara and Pete."

"Hhrrmmfff."

Clara received me awkwardly, allowing me to embrace her but not hugging back. Pete stood silently at her side.

"How are you holding up?" I asked.

She nodded, her thin, unpainted lips parting to say: "Fine." She reached for the tall cowboy beside her. "Have you met Pete?" she asked.

He removed his cowboy hat, mumbled, "Ma'am," and took my hand in his. I felt small and breakable in his grip. His face was puffy but his eyes were clear, not film-coated as I had imagined.

Clara was staring toward Donald. "What's he workin' on?" she asked suspiciously.

"He's giving the speech tonight," I told her.

Her eyes took on a cold, dark light. "Is that all?" She asked.

"What else?" I asked.

"I dunno. Maybe a poem. Maybe a deal to trick someone out of some land."

"No, just a speech," I said. I forgave Clara in my heart. She was under a lot of pressure with her father's disappearance. And because Donald is a part-time realtor, I hear a lot of jokes about land pirates.

Pete quieted Clara with a gentle arm about her shoulders. Their romance was one of those secrets that everyone had known about for years, yet they were seldom seen together in public.

"We ain't even found your pa yet," I heard Pete whisper. Clara coiled like a roll of barbed wire, then relaxed. "I'm sorry, Reba," she said.

I nodded.

"I had no call sayin' what I said. And thanks for the cards. And the books, I might even get around to readin' 'em."

A difficult moment followed. One that begged for a diversion. The diversion came. Dick and Marci entered the room.

Dick McColley, wandering cowboy. His wife, Marci, babe in Christ, my spiritual daughter. They rode in on Dick's wind with Marci in its wake. Dick is tall for a McColley, dark-haired and handsome with bright blue eyes set in clean, rugged features like pools of water in sandstone. Marci beamed like a prairie moon. She wore a sequined blouse, western slacks, and a heart-shaped silver belt buckle. Her blond hair tumbled to her shoulders. She was still rodeo-queen pretty.

They were not the diversion I had hoped for. Dick muttered a hello to me and Clara, then pulled Pete toward the portable bar in the back. He wanted a drinking companion, and Pete would do. Marci gave me a fierce, breathtaking hug. When I opened my eyes, Clara was gone.

"I'm starved for fellowship," Marci said, and began leading me toward the nearest chair. I looked around but could not see Clara. Donald was bent over his speech. Dick and Pete were already holding drinks.

"I brought all your books and tapes back," Marci said. "I hope you brought me some new ones. I can get a Christian radio station when the weather's right. I listen to Dobson and Swindoll. I found a church. It's thirty miles from the ranch. Dick only lets me go once a week, or less." She was a dry sponge, and I was water.

"I hope there's something in Donald's speech about the Lord," she continued. "I'm using anything I can to get Dick's attention. I've even left tracts in his pickup."

I was accustomed to Marci's exuberance but not ready for it tonight. She frequently wrote me long letters filled with spiritual questions. She phoned only when she was desperate.

"I'm talking too much," she said. "I can't help it. It's so good to see you. I hope we can find time to pray together. Dick wants to go straight home after the dinner. Can you believe that? It's 160 miles to Plentywood. Have you read Benny Hinn? What do you think of him? I read *This Present Darkness*. You were right. It's great. It makes me want to pray . . ."

She stopped midsentence and stared over my shoulder toward the door. "I can't believe he's here," she said.

I turned slowly. Warren McColley, Dick's older brother, stood in the doorway like an apparition.

"He's divorced now, isn't he?" Marci asked.

"Yes," I said. And he looked divorced. Divorced from his wife, his family, from life itself. He stood with his arms folded across his chest scanning the room as if it were a cave filled with ghosts. He wore a sport shirt, slacks, and black Reeboks. He was looking for Dick and I saw him home in on his brother's bell-like laughter. Its timbre must have resonated in his memory. It had been twenty years since he had left home, ten since returning for his mother's funeral. He did not come back for his father's.

I asked Marci to excuse me and went to greet him.

Behind the pain and guardedness his hazel eyes shone with intelligence. "Hello, Reba," he said and politely took my hand.

"It's good to see you, Warren."

"Your letters can be very persuasive," he said.

I welcomed him to come in.

"No. I need to stand for a minute," he said.

"It must be a bit of a shock being home after all these years," I said.

He agreed. "It's likely to be a strange evening."

"I saw my cousin Clara in the hallway," he said.

"This is hard for her," I told him. "Because of her father."

"She looks stressed," he said. "In fact, she looks like a fencepost with hair." Impulsively I gave him a chastening look. "I'm sorry," he said. "I'm always making snap critical judgments. Something to do with my ancestry, I think."

"Well," I said. "I'm sure you're anxious to see your brother."

"Maybe." He was staring across the room, not at Dick, but at a portrait of Alistair Angus McColley that hung beneath a spotlight on the wall. He focused intently, as if trying to stare the old man down. "Ironic, isn't it," he said. "That we would gather to honor a murderer?"

All I could do was clear my throat.

"Forgive me my defenses, Reba," he said, his eyes still locked on the painting. "Old wounds are rising, and here I am, a doctoral candidate in psychology, afraid of my own relatives."

"It would make for an interesting thesis," I joked.

He gave me a warm, but sly smile. "Indeed it does." He watched his remark settle. "I do want to talk to you later," he said, then began moving toward his brother.

Duty pulled me back to Donald who wants me near when he is troubled. I managed to placate Marci by pulling a small book from my handbag—Andrew Murray—and handing it to her. "Glance at this," I told her. "If you like it you can keep it."

Donald was concentrating so intently that his head almost glowed. Perhaps there was, after all, something to the rumor that his baldness was caused by his high-powered intellect. Donald's passion in life is work—he believes a man is defined by his labor—and work has kept him slim. Me, I depend on walks with friends and low-impact aerobic classes. Donald runs a real estate office full-time now that we have turned the farm over to our son, Donald, Jr. We also have a grown daughter, Donna, who lives in Denver. Besides work, Donald's other passions are writing cowboy poetry and doing projects at the lake cabin. It is our family retreat. I say that because it has caused our family to retreat.

I was attracted to Donald because I was young and vulnerable and he seemed strong and ambitious, but I married a scared, insecure child who covered his fears with arrogance. But I love him. His dry humor and practical common sense bring me to earth when I become too heavenly minded. He is bright and handy, capable of repairing anything. No appliance dies a natural death in our home.

I spend much of my time thinking about my marriage and praying for my husband. At that moment, as I sat beside him, I was thinking: *Donald, I know your mind, body, politics, and theology, but when will I know your heart?*

Then I felt a stirring beneath my ribs. I assumed it was a call to intercession and began to quietly pray in tongues, careful that Donald would not hear. My heavenly language angers him.

The warm oil of anointing began to flow. Then an incredible thing happened. My mind seemed to quicken, and my senses sharpened. My Lord's peace gripped me, otherwise I might have panicked.

And then I heard His voice.

My people are like books, He told me. *They have stories that are read and stories that go unread. If you will listen and not judge, the unread will be told.*

"Is that You, Lord?" I whispered.

Hear the story of the seed, taste of the fruit born from bitter roots.

The peace of His presence grew stronger as if He knew I was fearful. And then I heard a voice, soft and childlike, from beside me. It was Donald. I turned to him, but he was not speaking. He was still bent over his speech. I strained to hear, and the voice responded as if in a chamber of my mind. My Donald. Sharing his heart.

And this is what he said . . .

2
The Poet

I would like to write you a poem, Grandpa.
I wrote you one once, but you never knew. I was
eleven years old and herding sheep for you on
Mizpah Creek. When the sheep bedded down I climbed
a high hill and sat in the shade of a "sheepherder's wife,"
the rock monuments that old-time herders built as a sign
of water. I had a pencil and sketch pad with me, and I
drew the scene below me and began to compose my first
poem.

It was about you, Grandpa Alistair. You were a legend
in my young mind. Everyone talked about you. I was
finishing the second stanza when the writing paper flew
out of my hands. The sheets rose into the air and
scattered like a flock of pigeons. You stood above me,
your cedar walking stick in your hand and your dog,
Queenie, at your side. "Watch ye be doin', boy?" you
snapped.

I can still taste the fear as I scrambled to my feet. "N-n-nothin'," I said. "Just writin' a poem."

"A poem! Aye, we got a Robert Burns here, do we? What nonsense be ye writin' about laddie?"

Your tattered felt hat shaded your leathery face but I can still see the glow of your angry eyes. How could I tell you I was writing about you? I lied. "God," I said. "I was writin' a poem about God." I thought God would be a large enough wall to hide behind. I was wrong.

"God! You been hearin' fool ideas from your grandma?"

"No," I said, lying again.

"Then it's your ma, Duncan's woman. Always the women."

I shook my head, Grandpa, but you did not notice.

"Let me tell ye somethin', laddie. Churches and God ain't good for nothin' 'cept marriages and funerals. And meetin' women. Religion is a grief and a curse. It keeps men poor and arguin' about things they can't even see. You understand me, boy?"

I nodded.

"When I left the Old Country I vowed no offspring of mine would darken the doorway of a church except for one reason: to find a wife. You ready to get married, laddie?"

"No," I said.

You barely had to bend to put your face in mine. I can still smell the tobacco on your breath. "Is Jesus God?" you asked.

I froze with fear. My ma and grandma had said He was. I said nothing.

"Look at the woolies," you said, pointing your cedar stick toward the flock. "You let them bed in the thistles. Now their wool is matted with burrs."

"I-I-I'll move 'em," I said.

"Aye, you will move them laddie. But now let me ask you this: If Jesus is God and He is such a shepherd, why doesn't He move them for you? No, you have to do it for yourself." You pointed to a long white scar that ran from your scalp to below your left eye. "How did I get this?" you asked.

"Fightin' a badger," I said.

"Aye, in the thirties when food was scarce. I kilt me a mess o' sage hens and was sittin' under a rock cleanin' 'em when the badger dropped right down in me lap and went to eatin' the bird in me hands. And what did I do?"

"You threw the badger off."

"Aye, but not before he got his own licks in. Now where was God then?"

I wanted to say, "Maybe He had His hand over your eye." But I said nothing.

"How many toes have I got, laddie?"

"Uh, six," I said.

"That's right. I had four cut off from frostbite, the winter of '49, walkin' through drifts taller than me head. Where was God then? Aye, I tell ye, laddie, he is a figment in the minds of old women and preachers who are after your dollar."

"You don't believe in Him at all?" I asked.

"Believe? I believe in what I can hold in me hands, like me cedar stick, me good dog, money. I grew up force-fed on God and listenin' to arguments 'bout religion. Me pa was a Cat'o'lick. Me ma a follower of Knox." You shook your head and a veil of sadness covered your anger. "Aye, no God at all is better than a God cut up and put in different pens. No, laddie. I don't believe in God.

"And I don't believe in poems and such. Poems and religions are for dreamers. They won't put bread on your table, laddie. A man is made by his work, by the sweat of his brow, by the rattle in his belly. Do ye want to be a McColley, laddie?"

"Uh?" was all I could say.

"Do ye want to be a McColley?"

"Yes."

You touched your cedar stick upon my shoulder as if knighting me. "Then forgo all foolishness. Forget poems and religion and God. Work hard. Carve your own life. Ye promise?"

"I promise," I said.

"Aye, then ye will make a McColley someday. Now ye get about movin' me sheep outa those thistles."

You walked away. A small wiry man with a dog at his side and a staff in his hand. A prophet leaving the mountain. An apostle of atheism. I rousted the sheep from their beds. I worked hard. I did it. There was no one to help me. I bunched them and started them on the trail home. At sunset I turned and stared back at the high hill where the "sheepherder's wife" stood like an altar. On the sides of the hill the pages of my poem reflected the dying light. I watched them glow even after the sun had set. Then they flickered like candles. The light went out.

I tried to write you a poem, Grandpa.

I would write you one now. An epic of a man who came to America from Scotland when he was thirteen and worked his way to the West. A man who followed a herd of wethers up the Powder River into Montana and stayed, going back to Scotland once to claim a bride. A man who sired four children but saw the two daughters die. A man who carved a small empire from gumbo and hardpan while battling drought, blizzards, wolves, coyotes, and the Big Swede. A man who made his fortune, then returned it to the soil, somewhere in this vast expanse of prairie and badlands.

I would like to write you a poem, Grandpa. But there is a blockage in my soul. It is like a huge boulder in a stream. I can feel the splash and push of the water against it. The boulder is a rock from your mountaintop, Grandpa. From the hill where the pages of my first poem flickered like lanterns in the wind. It is a boulder of dense yellow rock, and it holds the words that were never spoken, the poems never written, songs never sung, and treasure never unearthed. The water splashes against the boulder, but the rock does not move. I am dammed. Forever dammed.

When Donald's voice ceased I was overwhelmed by the Lord's love for my husband and filled with a wonderful new hope and joy. I credited the experience to a deepened level of personal intercession made possible by the oneness of our marriage. In God's eyes, we were one flesh. I had access to Donald's heart. I expected my experience to end there, with Donald, and I saw him in a new light as a crushed child whose spirit was barricaded behind the stone walls of childhood trauma and deep inner vows. I wanted to hug him, hold him, wash his face with my tears. But all I could do was ask: "How is the speech coming along?"

"Stumbling on down the trail," he said.

I hit the hard, cold reality. "You will do fine," I said. Then I felt a hand on my shoulder. I turned, having no idea who to expect. It was Warren.

"I'm doing the social thing," he said. "You know, making table calls."

Donald looked up with knit brows.

"I understand you are giving the speech," Warren said.

"Yes," he said. "I am. How are you doing, Warren?" Their handshake happened just inches from my face. It emanated coolness.

"Me? I'm fine, fine. Still employed. Recently single. Not much else."

"At least you are still employed," Donald said.

"And you? Still in the land game?"

I felt Donald bristle. Land was decidedly not a game to Donald. He nodded.

"And I understand you are trying your hand at a little writing?"

He stiffened noticeably. Donald never *tried* anything. He *did* things. "Actually," he said, "I have had some fair success. Several livestock papers have published my work, and I have a book coming out this summer."

Warren's eyebrows lifted in subtle mockery. "A book? What type?"

"Poetry."

"Who is the publisher?"

"I'm going to publish it myself."

"Oh," said Warren. "A vanity book. Well, good luck. Who knows, the next thing we know you might be a guest on the 'Tonight Show.'"

"I hope to be," Donald said seriously. "Johnny Carson has had cowboy poets on. If Jay Leno has any sense, he will too."

"I know. I have seen them."

"Carson and Leno?"

"No, Donald. The cowboy poets on the show."

"Oh, do you follow cowboy poetry, Warren?"

"Hardly. I am simply a veteran of lonely, sleepless nights. Actually, I do read a lot of fiction. Mostly Montana writers at that. You know, the guys that live around Livingston and Missoula." He mentioned several names.

Donald shook his head. "Can't say I've heard of them," he said. "I can't imagine them writing cowboy stuff. There aren't any cowboys around Missoula. Just a bunch of long-haired, pot-smoking socialist professors."

"I don't think you would, uh, like the writers I read," Warren said.

"I like good ballads. Poems you can build a song out of. You say you've seen those guys on the 'Tonight Show'?"

"Yes, I did."

"I thought they did quite well," Donald said proudly, claiming them as peers. "The audience really seemed to be laughing with them."

"That's odd," Warren said. "I thought the audience was laughing at them."

The hinges of Donald's jaw tightened. Warren's lips parted into a thin, cynical smile. I drilled him with my eyes. *How could you be like Alistair and knock the pages from the hands of a child?*

Warren became aware of me but refused to meet my eyes. "Well," he said quickly. "I still haven't made it over to see Dickie. What has he been doing lately? Where has he been living?"

"Don't ask me," Donald said. "How that brother of yours manages to make a living is beyond me. Last I heard he was on some cow outfit in Nevada."

"He and Marci live near Plentywood," I said.

"Dickie the drifter," Warren said, affecting a western drawl. "Well, I guess I'll mosey on over and say howdy."

"Mosey all you want," Donald said. Warren moved away. "There goes a good argument against college education," Donald said.

"He's just uncomfortable right now," I said. I watched Warren approach his brother. A master's degree in Reeboks meeting a Stetson and Wranglers. As I watched, a cold chill entered my heart and a voice whispered, "Murder."

Murder? I wondered.

"Donald?" I asked. "Did you decide to mention the Big Swede?"

"You told me not to."

"I know. I was just wondering."

"Do you think I should?"

"No. Donald, Warren saw the murder, didn't he?"

"It wasn't murder, Reba. The jury ruled it as self-defense. You know that. And you know Warren saw it. He was the only witness."

"Murder," a voice said again.

Warren, I guessed. Warren saw more than he told. I centered my attention on Warren.

"Frustration," the voice said.

Frustration?

I was staring at Warren but suddenly he left my field of vision and was replaced by the smiling, clean-faced cockiness of his younger brother.

Dick?

Dick. And then I heard his story unfold.

3
The Rooster

I don't like places where there's no one for me to talk to so that's why I'm talkin' to Pete Andraxie. We could end up roaring drunk, but Pete says he's reformed and he's just drinkin' grapefruit juice. Somethin's got to 'im. Either Clara or religion, I suppose.

Who else is there to talk to?

Forget cousin Donald. Doggone federally subsidized sodbuster. Thinks he's a cowboy poet. Well, that's Donald, a legend in his own mind.

Clara? What do you say to a cousin who fears that the bones of her old man are being packed around by coyotes? I'd say the wrong thing, you can count on that.

Then there's my long-lost brother, Warren. I seen him come in, but he doesn't know it yet. Caught his lost, gaunt-lookin' face in the mirror. What do I talk to him about? I don't understand any of that psycho-babble.

He doesn't even look like anybody I know. Too skinny and losin' his hair. Looks like a vegetarian environmentalist. The funny thing is, he's startin' to resemble Dad. Or even Grandpa Alistair. And he's carryin' that haunted look of the recently divorced. What was her name? Linda? Somethin' like that.

I've never really known my brother, I just know we're different. But I always respected him for his intelligence and education. He did what I never had the discipline to do. He writes me occasionally but I never answer. Writin' isn't my thing. Besides, we never had anything in common except basketball. And then I was always better at it than him but liked it less.

Maybe I should talk to him. Get him over in a corner and say, "Brother, I want to talk to you about Pa."

And he would say something like: "Look, Dick, I missed Dad's funeral and I missed Grandpa's, but at least I'm here now." Warren has always had a thing about guilt. He wears it like a brand.

And I would say: "Naw, man. The thing is I *killed* Dad. You're the shrink. Let's talk about it."

And I did. Kill Dad, that is. I don't know if I meant to or not. But I won't really talk to Warren about it. I do my talkin' in my head, not with my lips.

I worked for the Rooster half a dozen times after getting back from Nam. I never lasted more than a year. He'd have some fit or something—or I would— and I'd get fired or quit. A year or two later, we'd try it again.

His name was Roland, he was Grandpa Alistair's oldest boy, but everyone called him the Rooster. He got that handle 'cuz he'd boxed bantamweight a little bit when he was young. Also, 'cuz he was like a little bantie rooster, full of cock, crow, and strut. Never weighed more than 120 pounds soakin' wet and stood about five-four. Me, I'm a little over six foot and I think that rankled him. Everyone always told me when I was growin' up that to understand my father or my uncle Duncan you had to know their pa. The famous Alistair Angus McColley.

Heck, I knew Grandpa. I liked him. He was gruff but he spoke his mind. And he didn't just talk. He did what he talked about.

Like killing the Big Swede. A lot of little hotheads can strut around sayin' they're gonna kill someone, but Grandpa up and done it. Now I'm not for killing people, I saw enough of that overseas, but if a man gets pushed he's gotta push back, and Grandpa would push back.

He was foul-mouthed and over-fed on opinions. Tended to smell bad, too. He always wore wool pants and long-handled underwear, winter or summer. "What keeps the cold out keeps the hot out," he'd say. And just as bad, he usually had a border collie in his lap, a dog that had gas from eatin' rotten mutton. Queenie was her name, and when she broke wind, she would look over at me and smile, her tongue hangin' out. Grandpa never said a word or rolled his window down. There could have been a bouquet of roses growin' outa that seat as far as he was concerned.

Actually, I liked ridin' around with Grandpa. It was ridin' around with my dad I couldn't take. If there is such a thing as hell, it's bein' in the pickup with the Rooster, him drivin', and the radio on. Him and his endless radio.

Come winter, Dad and I fed cattle way out in the hills instead of close to home on better grass and water. "They gotta make a livin' on their own," he'd spout, so we would spend every morning drivin' through the badlands cakin' each little bunch as we found 'em and breakin' water in the ponds. He treated his cows like wildlife and that's how they acted.

Ol' Roland, he always had to drive. Said he liked for me to open the gates. He just liked bein' in control. Always had the radio on real loud so he could listen to the latest market and weather reports. I swear, a cloud couldn't fly overhead without him havin' to hear about it on the radio. That old truck had a great radio, too. Grandpa Alistair was always tellin' him to buy trucks that was plain on the outside but full of fancy on the inside. That way strangers wouldn't suspect you had any money and be devicin' a way to separate you from it. Grandpa stamped his brand of opinion on his offspring, that's for sure.

I did all the hard choppin' at the water holes, and the Rooster would take the shovel and skim the ice chunks out all the while complainin' my holes weren't big enough or were too close together. Always crowin'.

Then we'd bunch the cows on a feed ground and he'd drive while I shoveled the feed pellets outa the back of the truck. He'd sit inside, the radio blarin', countin' my scoops to make sure I didn't feed the cows too much. He could hardly see over the steerin' wheel so he was always hittin' badger holes and washouts. Throwed me right out on the ground once. My back hasn't been the same since, it pains me somethin' constant.

And pee! That's another thing. The ol' Rooster had to get out and pee about thirty times a mornin'. I never knew if his bladder was bad or if he was just markin' his territory like some old dog coyote.

Marci could never understand me comin' back so often and workin' for him. Lots of abuse for $500 a month and a two-bit trailer house to live in. Guess I couldn't understand it either, but he was my pa. They say a buck deer usually dies a few miles from where it was born. The pull of the familiar, I guess.

He always took us back without a word. Whoever was workin' in my place was fired, and we'd move back into the trailer. Marci would complain for a week but then get used to it. What bothered her most was the Rooster never called her by her name. It was always "her" or "your woman" or "hey you." She thought it was very disrespectful. Probably was. I just laughed and told her that hey-you sounded Chinese and asked her where the blond hair came from.

"The worst thing about your dad," she would fire back, "is that you are so much like him." Well, I ain't now, I guess. Cuz he's dead.

The thing about me killin' him—if I did—it was only just a game. Just givin' him back a little of his own orneriness. It surprises me now that I did it. I've always thought of myself as being more direct than that. Heck, I don't even know what got me playin' games with Dad, but I know it started simple enough. One day I noticed he had trouble getting the shovel out of the back of the pickup when it bounced into the middle of the bed. So I started nudgin' it there just to make him hop and sweat a bit. Every water hole we stopped at I saw to it that his shovel was just outa his reach.

I've always tried to have fun. Life gets awful slow otherwise. When I was a drinker, the jokes would sometimes get out of hand. Sometimes the things I did surprised me. Like the deal with that black guy.

And this deal with Dad and the shovel, I regret the heck out of it, but what can I do about it now? If the Rooster had a heart condition he never told anyone about it, and I've never been old, so I tend to forget what it must be like.

Now I look across the room at Warren and see traces of the old man, like the Rooster had crawled outa the grave and growed a little more hair.

A man should know why his dad died, but I don't know that I can tell Warren. What would I say? Warren, I played a little joke with a shovel and it killed Dad.

Shovels. It seems we McColleys have got a thing about shovels. That's how Grandpa killed the Big Swede.

At first the shovel prank seemed comical. As I chopped ice, he'd be strainin' and reachin' to get to it and cursin' up a cloud as blue as diesel smoke. At any time he could have asked for a hand, but the old man was never one to ask for help, especially not from me. Heck, I couldn't help it he was born short.

As he huffed and puffed and hopped about, I'd chop away and think about all the dang feed I'd shoveled for him. He bought his cake by the semi-load, and we'd auger it into an old railroad car, then every evening I'd shovel a ton of it into the back of the truck. Now each scoop weighs about twenty pounds, so that's 100 shovelsful of cake every morning. Then I'd have to shovel it off as we fed. So that's two tons of shovelin' a day. And me with a bad back after gettin' throwed outa the truck.

There's other ways we could have done it. They sell these tall, free-standing silos now where you auger the feed in, then you drive your truck under 'em, pull a trap door, and let it gravity-fill. But they would cost the Rooster some money.

So two tons a day, startin' about the first of December and goin' to the first of May. That's five months. One hundred and fifty days. Three hundred tons a winter. And how many winters was there? All of them from the time Warren left until I joined the Marines. That was five. Then I came home for two more. Got married. Got fired. Rehired. Quit. In all, I suppose I worked twelve full winters.

That's thirty-six hundred tons of feed.

That's what I figured in my head while the old man hopped and puffed and I chopped away, my sciatica blazing like fire.

Seven million, two hundred thousand pounds. That's
what it comes to, and that's what I was thinkin' the day
I heard the huffin', puffin', and the hoppin' quit.

One moment it was a cold, still winter day. Temperature was about twenty below, but the sun was out so it
felt warmer. I was even workin' up a good sweat
swingin' that ax. The Rooster's hoppin' and puffin' was
just background noise, somethin' that came to my ear
in between blows to the ice. Then there was silence. I
don't mean just the lack of the hoppin' and cussin', but
real silence.

I lifted up my head, the sweat stingin' my eyes, and
there was the ol' Rooster layin' in the snow, like a coat
someone had throwed under the truck. He'd fallen
quietly, like a scarf settling down out of the breeze.

Dead just looks dead. You can see a horse sleeping
on its side and your mind says it might be dead, but when
you really see somethin' dead, you know it. I looked up
from that stock pond and didn't even consider running
to him to help. He had dead written all over him, and
it's odd, but instead of feeling grief or shame, my mind
wanted to joke about it.

Doggone, I thought, he just huffed and puffed till he
broke. I walked up and turned the radio off, then picked
up the little man and put him in the passenger seat. I
pulled his cap down firm on his head and leaned him
against the door like he was restin'. I even took a
moment to close his eyes for him so he just wouldn't be
gazin' at nothing. Then for the first time, I drove us
home.

As we neared the house we came to a fenceline with a particularly bothersome wire gate. "You mind gettin' the gate?" I asked.

He didn't feel up to it, so I got it.

That gate was always hard to open but never more so than that morning. As I put my arm around the cedar post and hugged it tight, a rush of thoughts came flooding through my mind. The first was what to tell Marci. She usually knows when I'm avoidin' the truth. Then what would happen to the ranch? I didn't know if the old man had a will. Maybe it would be a chance for Marci and me to have a place of our own. Then I thought about Warren and the phone call I would have to make. I'd be real factual, like I was callin' the grain elevator about the price of oats. But mostly my back hurt as I arched into the gatepost, and that got me thinkin' about all the feed I'd shoveled. Now all of this is happenin' in a flash, quick thoughts like when a horse blows up and bucks.

Maybe all that shoveled feed was the unbearable burden, somethin' bound to break me or Dad. The thought left as quick as it came, like fog from a windshield when you turned the heater on.

I got back in the truck and the Rooster was sittin' there restin' like someone had finally turned his radio off. "Where do you suppose Grandpa's gold is?" I asked. He didn't volunteer an answer.

So now it's a question of who do I tell what. Ain't talked much about it to anyone, except a little to Marci. Guess my last good words were to Pa.

"Seven million, two hundred thousand pounds," I told him as we drove into the ranchyard. "Now that's a lot of shovelin'." I hit a bump and his head nodded as if to say, "It sure is."

And it is. Seven million, two hundred thousand pounds is quite a burden to bear.

Murder. I felt stained, defiled by the blood-guiltiness of Dick McColley's crime. I had briefly become a part of him, settling to the deep reaches of his soul where his anger boiled like a cauldron of lava. As it rose to the surface the anger subsided into layers of superficial charm, humor, and worldly integrity.

I glanced across the room at him. He was smiling boyishly as he talked with Pete Andraxie. If Dick was burdened with guilt, he did not show it. I wondered if he had really done what I had heard, or was my mind playing tricks on me?

I was anguished for Marci. What was it like being a Christian woman married to a man so suppressed by anger and frustration? Now I knew what it was like.

I needed air. No. I did not want to go outside. I needed to stand. To walk. I nudged Donald. "Sweetheart," I said, "can I get you something?"

He grunted. It was an affirmative grunt.

"Coffee?" I asked.

He grunted again. He was on the third stanza of his epic poem.

The caterers in the kitchen were busy. I went to the portable bar knowing it would bring me close to Dick. I felt a mixture of curiosity and repulsion.

Warren, Dick, and Pete were standing at the bar. Dick was doing the talking. I asked the bartender for coffee, and he said he had to brew a fresh pot. I waited. I wasn't trying to be nosy but I couldn't help hearing the men talking.

"So, big brother, how's life?" I heard Dick ask. "You still working with troubled boys?"

"Yes," Warren said. "I am in the Cascades a lot. At a remote mountain camp." I could sense he was trying to explain why he had not attended his father's funeral. I huddled myself like a sparrow in a snowstorm. I watched for the bartender. I tried not to overhear but the conversations seemed amplified.

"Hear you got divorced," Dick said.

"Yes. Yes, I did."

"Too bad. What was her name? Linda, wasn't it?"

"Marge."

"Marge?"

"Yes. Marge."

Dick shrugged. "That's odd, I always thought it was Linda."

"It doesn't make any difference. She changed it."

"You mean the whole name? Not just the McColley part?"

"Shaulitta Starlight." Warren said flatly.

Dick spat tobacco into an empty beer can. "What the heck, did she become a stripper or somethin'?"

"No. A channeler."

"Channeler? What's that?"

"A psychic."

"You mean like a mindreader or somethin'?"

Pete raised his eyes from his drink and looked at Warren suspiciously. Warren glanced at him, and Pete's vision returned to the bar. Pete turned away to give the brothers privacy and our eyes met. We both looked down, embarrassed.

"Mindreader?" Warren said. "Sort of. Only stranger."

"Reminds me of Magic," Dick said.

"Well, it is a little like magic—"

"No. The bird. Magic the Magpie. Remember?"

"Oh." Warren's head tilted as if rolling his eyes backward into memory. "The bird. I had forgotten all about that bird."

"The only thing I've ever known that can read minds," Dick said, "are magpies. They fly in to steal food from the dog dish, and you can walk right by them unarmed and they pay you no mind. But the moment you even think about grabbing a shotgun they are on the wind. Mindreaders."

Dick had made me feel like a magpie.

"And our father had one . . .," Warren said.

"Magic. I caught it when it was young, and Dad split its tongue so it could talk."

"He had it in a cage on the porch, didn't he?"

"Yup. Every morning for a year I woke up to him coachin' that bird to speak. But it never would. He'd get mad and yell: 'Burn in blazes, you dumb bird.' That always put the Rooster in a bad mood for the rest of the day."

"So it never talked?" Warren said.

Dick laughed. "Oh, it talked. The summer you worked for Grandpa. The year he killed the Big Swede. The Rooster finally gave up and turned ol' Magic loose. Surprised me, I figured he'd just kill it. Anyway, about a week later we were brandin' calves in the corral . . ."

"The day the Rooster lost his thumb," Warren said.

"That's right. He double-hocked a big calf, and got his thumb caught takin' his dally. He never could rope worth a lick. The thumb popped off at the joint, and Mom tried to make us all stop and look for it convinced that doctors could sew it back on. The Rooster wanted to keep on workin' but this one time Mom got her way. So we all started scratchin' in the dust for Dad's thumb."

Warren's coffee had grown cold in his hands. He set the cup down. "This is one of those tales with a moral at the end, isn't it?" he asked.

"Could be. All stories have some sorta moral, I suppose. Anyway, we were all on our hands and knees like it was some sorta prayer meetin', the Rooster still horseback crowin' at us to get back to work when ol' Magic came flyin' in." Dick paused for effect. "Ol' Magic," he continued, "lit right in the corral, hopped about three hops, pecked somethin' outa the dust, and flew up on a corral post."

"Dad's thumb?"

"Right as rain. And Dad started nudgin' his big bay up toward that post. 'Here, Magic,' he was sayin', 'be a good bird.' And that bird curled its feet around the thumbtip, looked the Rooster in the eye and squawked: 'Burn in blazes! Dumb bird!' Then he flew away takin' the thumb with him."

Warren rolled his eyes.

"You think I'm makin' this up?" Dick asked.

"Aren't you?"

"Heck, I dunno," Dick said. "If it's my lie, I can tell it anyway I want. I'm just surprised you don't remember it."

"There is a lot I have chosen to forget," Warren said.

"That could be," Dick said, "but anyways, you started the mindreadin' talk by mentioning Linda—"

"Marge."

"Whatever. Shawnee Sunshine or whatever she calls herself. Anyway, I was wondering. Can you psychologists read minds?"

"What?" Warren's professionalism was offended. "Read minds?"

"Yeah. When people aren't telling you the whole story, can you read what's being left out?"

"Well, I suppose there are times when I feel like I am inside someone's head. Why do you ask?"

"Oh, no reason," Dick said. "I was just wondering if you knew what was in my head."

Warren gave his younger brother a confused look. "Dick, I don't have a clue what's in your head."

Dick turned slightly and stared vacantly at the wall. I knew what he knew: he was hearing the Rooster, huffing, puffing, falling. "Good," Dickie said softly.

The bartender brought me Donald's coffee. I turned to walk away when a new voice began speaking softly in the back of my mind. I needed to get to my chair. It was too hard to listen and walk at the same time. "Satan," I whispered, "if this is you and not the Spirit, then I rebuke you in the name of Jesus, and I command the voice to stop."

The voice became slightly louder, like a long-distance phone call when the static has cleared.

I strained to hear. It was long distance. It was Oregon.

It was Warren.

4
The Pure Shooter

It is a long drive from Eugene, Oregon, to Yellow Rock, Montana. I did it in two miserable days spent thinking first of Marge and basketball. Then, as the plains of eastern Montana approached, my thoughts turned to my father and grandfather. I crossed the Continental Divide knowing I was on an icy slide from the lush intellectual and cultural environs of the northwest to the barren narrow-mindedness of sagebrush and prairie.

I nearly turned back while filling my Miata with gas in Billings. No one expected me, no one would miss me. But in reaching for my wallet I pulled out a letter I thought I had thrown away. I read it again. Reba explained that my grandpa Alistair had passed away in a nursing home in Yellow Rock.

"I hope this letter gets to you," it read. "I have tried calling, but your old number is disconnected." Reba had not known about the divorce, about Marge moving back to Portland and me into a less expensive apartment.

"The day Alistair passed away," she continued, "Uncle Duncan disappeared in a blizzard. He has not yet been found."

What are the chances, I wondered, of a hundred-year-old man and his seventy-something son dying on the same day?

"I know it has been a tough year," she said. "Beginning with your father's death last winter."

A funeral I did not attend, she could have added.

"Grandpa is being inducted in the Pioneer Museum Hall of Fame in April," she wrote. "Can you make it?"

The Pioneer Hall of Fame? Marge would have found that appropriate. To her all pioneers were murderers. Northern European exploiters. And Grandpa was a murderer, wasn't he?

Call it curiosity or guilt, but I decided to go. I had nothing to lose. Marge was gone, and my tumultuous world was further shaken by a long-limbed, red-headed basketball player. The greatest shooter I had ever seen.

It is not unusual for a newly divorced man to be obsessed with thoughts of his ex. But a basketball player?

Basketball was culture on the plains of Montana. There was no symphony, no ballet, just small, drafty gyms that doubled as meeting centers and dance halls.

Our ranch was thirty-five miles from Yellow Rock. My grade school was a one-room shack with an attached teacherage and a coal furnace that roared for constant feeding. High school brought me to Yellow Rock and introduced me to organized sports.

My father, the Rooster, hated basketball. He wanted me home weekends to work. But my junior year, my mother convinced him to let me play. Because of my long, arching, one-handed set shot, I made varsity my senior year.

I left Yellow Rock as soon as I graduated. Dick entered high school and played ball while still finding time to work on the ranch. He was a starter on the varsity squad his sophomore year. My mother sent clippings that I posted in my dorm room. I told my friends that Dick and I were very close. Of course we weren't, but I wanted to think so.

Then the clippings stopped coming. I told my friends Dick was on a full-ride at Kansas. But he wasn't even in college. He was in the Marines. In Viet Nam. I wrote him in Saigon but he never answered.

I put Montana behind me. I studied psychology, married Marge, got a job as a counselor, played pickup ball games, got divorced. Played more ball.

At first I paid no attention to the sound. I had heard it so often before: the rhythmic, hollow slapping of a basketball on the floor of a wooden court. But then I detected its sister sound, as cadenced as a heartbeat: the sweet rippling swish of a ball passing rimlessly through nylon netting.

I left the coach at his desk and moved to the tiny window that looked down on the gym. Below me was a lone figure—I guessed him my age—shooting jump shots from the top of the key. Only shooting was not the word. The man was a dancing machine. Each movement sang of sweet efficiency.

"He's something, isn't he?" the coach said.

I agreed and asked his name.

"The name's Cremer," the coach told me.

I could not take my eyes off him. The coach continued working on the proposed schedule that I had brought for the city's Over-Thirty Recreational Basketball League. "What is his story?" I asked.

"He comes in every day," the coach said. "But he doesn't like being watched."

I pulled back a ways from the window. "Why not?"

"He's had his share of crowds."

I asked for more, but my eyes did not leave the miniature silhouette that spun magic on the softly glistening hardwood.

"First-team All-State his junior year," I heard the coach say. "Then he killed his girlfriend in a car wreck that shattered his shooting arm."

The shots kept dropping in, one after another, the net constantly rippling, barely settling before another ball made the webs sing. I sensed a purpose in the shooter and began counting softly under my breath. The coach heard me.

"He does the same thing every day," the coach said. "He shoots his fifty."

"Shoots his fifty?"

"Fifty shots from the top of the key," the coach said. "I think his goal is to hit fifty straight."

I watched Cremer in awe. Since college I had played year-round in the city leagues, regularly watched the college team, and traveled to Portland to see the Trail-blazers. I was a basketball nut. Basketball was my religion. But I had never seen a shooter like this.

"I know what you are thinking," the coach said. "You want to get him on your team in your old man's league." I nodded. "Forget it," he said. "He won't play."

But I had to find out. I excused myself, telling the coach I would return for the schedule, and got to the gym floor as the shooter was pulling on his sweats to leave. Close up he was taller, harder, and leaner. He did not seem surprised to see me.

"My name is Warren McColley," I told him. "I have a team in the Over–Thirty League and I was wondering if you would be interested in playing."

I offered my hand but he didn't take it. I noticed that his left arm was lined with a spider web of scars. "Thanks," he said, "but I don't play." His voice was flat but without malice. It was simply a fact. A finality. He did not play. He slung his court shoes over his shoulder and strolled away catlike—long-limbed, supple, and strong—a sorrowful, angry energy radiating from every fiber and vein of his being. He seemed capable of either great artistry or violence. He fascinated me.

I had to know more about him. The next day I went to the newspaper morgue and spent hours researching past basketball seasons. He had lived in a neighboring town and as a junior had been recruited by every major school in the country. Indiana, UCLA, North Carolina, De Paul. Holy places. Shrines. Every game account began with his name. His statistics filled the box scores. He once scored sixty-eight points in a game. They called him Mitch Cremer, the Oregon Maravich.

I found the newspaper account of the accident. There were two photographs of him on the front page. One showed him driving to the basket during a game. An inset photo was his junior class picture. And hers. She was pretty in a naive, suburban way. The story listed her activities: French Club, cheerleading. The article carried to the inside pages where there was a nighttime photo of what once had been a car. The photographer's strobe illuminated the tangled white Camaro in brilliant starkness to the darkness of the night.

At the school where I work I asked people about him. Most had seen him play. One had known his parents. No one remembered the name of the girl. That evening I mentioned him to the guys on my team. They all knew about him, or at least had heard the name.

I wondered why I hadn't. I remembered a conversation or two when reference had been made to a former great, a shooter, but I had assumed they were talking about a dead man.

He rode to the gym on a ten-speed. I learned to recognize the bike when it was in the rack and found excuses to visit the coach in his office.

"He knows you are up here," the coach told me one day. "He doesn't like you watching him. The dribble. He's dribbling harder than usual."

"You never watch him?" I asked.

"No. I just listen. He has been doing this for months now. Subconsciously I have learned to listen for a miss; the day I don't hear one I will know he will have finally hit his fifty."

"He's been close?"

"Forty-eight several times, forty-nine once that I know of."

"He is the best shooter I have ever seen," I said, aware that I had said this before.

"A pure shooter," the coach said. "He can hit from anywhere on the court."

"How good could he have been?" I asked.

"Unstoppable. If he played today they would have to move the three-point line out another three feet or so."

"But why the fifty?" I asked. Why did he come to the gym alone, day after day, trying to hit fifty baskets in a row from the top of the key?

"Don't ask me," the coach said. "You're the psychologist."

Once I followed him to the small apartment where he lived alone and to his job as a security guard at a manufacturing plant. I felt ashamed for my nosiness, and yet it was exciting. He is just a case, I told myself, not a person but a case study. I learned he took a night course at the college. Anatomy and physiology. He had just moved back to Eugene after working at a lumber mill in Washington. He made me forget Marge— Shaulitta Starlight—and her New Age channeling and crystals. Marge was a phony, a spoiled academic that had never experienced anything original in her life. Cremer was real, and yet he was far more mystical in his own way that my ex could ever hope to be.

Every day I looked for his bike in the rack outside the gym. But the weather turned against me, becoming windy and cool. He started running to the gym, his tall figure bundled in old sweats, the hood over his head. And worse, he began alternating shifts at his job. I never knew when he would be shooting.

"Would you call me and tell me?" I asked the coach.

"No, McColley, I can't do that," he said.

"How about a key?" I asked. "Would you mind if I had a key to the gym and your office?"

He gave me a dark, reducing scowl. "Don't you think you're carrying this a little too far?" he asked.

"I just want to be there," I told him, "when Cremer hit his fifty." I had been watching him for weeks and recording his results.

"Why?" the coach demanded. "What is your interest in this?"

I told him I wasn't sure. I told him I thought it was just a professional curiosity. I told him Cremer reminded me a little of my younger brother, Dick, only taller with red hair. "I guess I need to know what motivates him," I said.

"Why don't you just ask him?"

I didn't need to answer. The coach knew why. I was afraid of Cremer, and in his own way, I think the coach was too.

He had come to the gym for months, I reminded the coach. "You gave him a key. He shoots fifty a day, every day. Wouldn't you like to know why?"

"Did you know about the drinking?" the coach asked.

The drinking? The newspapers hadn't mentioned it.

Cremer had been drunk when he wrecked the car. He was hospitalized for a year.

The fifty shots . . . It had to be either absolution or meditation.

"What?" the coach asked.

"He's either trying to absolve himself of guilt," I explained, "or he uses the shooting as a meditation technique to combat the urge to drink. Maybe both."

"I suppose it is relaxing," the coach said. "Providing he is left alone. But what's with this absolution garbage?" he asked.

"Perfection," I said. "He is striving for a perfection—an improbable but not impossible one—to absolve himself of the pain he caused."

The coach shrugged. "Could be," he said. "But I doubt it."

"He is somehow strengthening a weakness, filling a void," I said.

"Have you ever noticed what arm he shoots with?" the coach asked.

Of course I had. The right.

"He used to be left-handed."

On the court below the lanky man went through his ritual dance. Three dribbles, then a slow-rising jumper, elbow in, quick release, follow through. Swish. A Barishnikov in Reeboks. Using his right hand, his weak member, he was as close to perfect as any man could be.

"Coach," I said. "Can I have the keys?"

"No," he said, "I have given you too much already."

I wanted to say: *But you gave Cremer a key.* The coach turned to me as if he knew what I was thinking, and I knew his thoughts: *But I trust Cremer more than I trust you.*

But I already had the keys, and I hated myself for it. I had palmed an extra set days before and had had copies made. The originals were back in the desk, the copies were in my pocket where they rubbed hot against my thigh like flint.

The coach took his team on an extended road trip. I dropped by the gym three, four times a day. If Cremer was there I let myself into the office and watched. Cremer was not doing any better. He was now hitting in the low forties.

I learned little new about him, but I was content to just watch from the coach's small office above the gym.

The coach almost caught me once. I was sitting in the corner when I heard the sound of a key in the door. Quickly I crawled under the desk and pulled my knees up to my chest. The light came on. I heard the coach rustling through mail on his desk. I prayed he would not sit down. How would I have explained myself? I imagined him lecturing me, even spanking me, reporting me to my superiors. I wondered if I would lose my license and be unable to counsel in the state. I was afraid to breathe.

Spanking me? Where had that come from? Why did I feel a need for the inner child to be punished?

A vision flashed through my mind. Cremer at the three-point line, raising the ball to shoot. The ball elongated, until it became a shovel. Cremer shrank and became my grandfather. He raised the shovel over his head. The sun glistened off the blade.

I heard the door close. The coach had left. I stayed under the chair curled in a fetal position for several minutes. I had not been that scared or that ashamed of myself since the summer I had turned twelve, the summer Grandpa killed the Big Swede. And I could see it all again. I was in the tiny guest room in the back of the house. My grandmother was in the kitchen making dinner. Mashed potatoes and roast lamb. I heard the angry argument pass barely muted through the thin walls of the old house. I went to the window and looked.

I tried staying away. I tried reasoning with myself. But I couldn't. I came back, night after night, day after day. Then one day I sensed it in my hands. The feeling. I was a shooter too. Not as good as Dick, and nowhere as good as Cremer. But a good shooter. Since seeing Cremer I had gone often to the gym alone to try to duplicate his form. Often I had taken fifty shots from the top of the key, and I was improving. From thirty-two, to thirty-five, to thirty-seven. I was gaining ground.

Once he came to the gym while I was shooting. I do not think he recognized me. He immediately left but returned hours later, and I was waiting for him, sitting quietly in the office corner, a few feet back from the window.

Then one morning I awakened with the sensation in my hands, the touch that tells you everything you throw up is going in. I imagined Cremer lived with that feeling, as certain as his skin, something that could not be rubbed or washed off. As real as a bloodstain. I called in sick for work and drove to the gym. And waited. I did not shoot or touch a ball. I was afraid the feeling would go away. It was after dark when he came in. I think he looked different, felt different too. He went through his warm-ups then walked straight to the line. Nineteen feet, nine inches to the rim. Swish, swish, swish. Nothing but net. I drew myself closer to the window. My palms were sweating. Swish, swish, swish. He was on automatic pilot, and I knew he was going to do it. On thirty-seven he was wide to the left. I held my breath and my body leaned with empathy, but he got the bounce and it rolled in. Five more passed through rimlessly. On forty-three, he was inches to the right but the topspin took the ball upwards, against the backboard, and it bounced down and through. A shooter's bounce. My breath was fogging the window, and I used my shirtsleeve to wipe it clean.

Forty-six, forty-seven, forty-eight.

Something was rising from deep within me as if I was suppressing a loud cheer.

Forty-nine . . . swish. The ball rolled to the far side of the court. He walked over, picked it up, and walked nonchalantly back to the line. He dribbled once, twice, three times. Then he stopped. He turned and looked up at the window. I could feel his eyes. I felt as if the glass was magnifying me and my face was twenty feet high and twenty feet wide. He raised his long left arm with the web of blue and white scars and pointed at me. With his right hand he pressed the ball down, onto the court, next to the line. Then he swept his left arm around and pointed at the ball.

"You!" he was saying. "You come down and shoot number fifty."

I drew back a few inches from the window.

He pointed again to me, then down to the ball.

You! You come down and shoot.

I felt his malice and accusations. Did he really want me to shoot? Did I dare step down to the floor?

He stood there for several minutes waiting to see if I would respond.

I could not. A cold sweat was drenching my shirt, and my hands were trembling. I was in no condition to shoot, no condition to shoot number fifty.

He waited a few moments more then walked off the court. I could sense his disgust. He left the ball sitting on the floor and deep sobbing erupted from my chest. I lowered my head and wept.

The ball was still there when I left the gym. One round, smooth, leather orb casting a long shadow toward the goal. I left the college quickly, the chilly

Oregon air freeze-drying the perspiration as I trotted to my car. That afternoon I got the letter from Reba. "Please try to come for Grandpa's induction," she said. "The family would love to see you."

I thought I heard the rhythmic, hollow sound of a ball bouncing in an empty gymnasium. The slow dribble became the sound of a heartbeat. The vacant gymnasium was the temple, the body of Warren McColley. The hollow, slapping cadence was the beat of his heart. I could see a small boy on the court, faintly lit by the light of a small window. He held a ball-sized heart in his hands and stared up at a circular rim that glowed softly, suspended in the air like an angel's halo. He was crying for confidence.

"Shoot it, Warren," I said.

"What did you say?" the voice jolted me back to the museum. It was Donald.

"Uh, nothing, I—"

"I'm missing some notes. I think I left them in my coat pocket."

"I'll get them," I said. I was eager to move. I rose from my chair, instinctively smoothing the wrinkles from my dress as if I could resolve my two worlds with a brush of my hand. To get to where the coats were hung, I had to pass through a jam of people standing around the bar. There were mostly old men holding drinks in frail and shaking hands. I tried to ease around them but was pressed against the backs of Warren and Dick. They did not notice. They were talking basketball.

"So, do you still play ball?" I heard Warren ask.

"Haven't played in years," Dick said. "The Rooster hit a badger hole and it tossed me out of the back of the truck. My back's never been the same."

"You were a great player," Warren said. "Mother sent me clippings, but why didn't you finish your senior year?"

Dick shrugged. "The coach caught me ridin' saddle broncs and told me to choose between basketball and rodeo."

"And how many scholarship offers did that cost you?" Warren asked.

Dick shrugged again. I could feel the texture of his shirt as his shoulders raised and lowered. "Six or seven," he said. There was no regret in his voice.

"I kept the clippings for years," Warren said. "I read them over and over. I think you were probably the second-best ball player I have ever known."

"I'll bite," said Dick. "Who was better?"

Warren told the story of Mitch Cremer, how he met him in the gym. He mentioned the car accident, the shattered shooting arm, and Cremer's dedication to hitting fifty straight.

"Did he ever do it?" Dick asked.

"Uh, you mean hit the fifty?"

Dick nodded.

"Uh, no, but I saw him hit forty-nine in a row once."

"Then he choked," Dick said.

"Uh, no," Warren paused. I wondered what he would admit to. "He wanted me to shoot it," he said.

"You? Why you?"

Warren lowered his head. "I don't know," he said.

"So, did you shoot the ball?"

"No," Warren said quickly. "I mean, how could I? He had been trying for months, maybe years. It was his pilgrimage. What if I had missed?"

Dick sipped from his beer. "I would have shot it," he said.

"But what if you had missed—"

Dick chuckled. "Then it would have been his fault," he said. "For handing me the ball."

Light appeared before me. An opening in the crowd. I slipped through, still thinking about the conversation and the difference between the two brothers. One tentative and introspective, the other superficial and cavalier. The difference, I realized, was not as great as it would appear.

I found Donald's notes and returned to the banquet hall. I glimpsed Marci trying to get my attention. I ignored her. I had enough on my mind without having to do fireside counseling. I wanted to spend time fellowshipping with her, but I wanted my strange revelations to end first. It was hard being in two worlds.

I heard her call my name.

I kept passing through the crowd.

"Reba," she called.

I stopped, resigned myself to duty, and turned around. Marci was sitting where I had left here. She was reading the Andrew Murray book. She was not looking at me.

"Reba," I heard her call again. But her head did not raise and her lips did not move.

I moved quickly to my chair, handed Donald his notes, and waited. And Marci began to speak.

5
My Husband

This place is beginning to feel like a funeral.

The whole setting is very strange. A ceremony honoring the memory of Alistair McColley? I'm glad they didn't ask me to speak. I can't say much about Alistair McColley because I don't believe in speaking ill of the dead. Besides, he never had much to do with me—I don't know if he even knew my name, I was just "Dickie's woman."

I know Dick seemed to think a lot of him. Dick hated sheep, but he respected Alistair because he was tough. He had a reputation.

I met Dick at the State High School Rodeo. He was the bronc rider on top of every barrel racer's list. So cocky. So swaggering. He just knew he was immune to injury or death—plus, his narrow hips and long, muscled legs looked great in a pair of Wranglers.

We married young, right after he got out of the Marines. We had such big plans. We were going to get our own little place and raise and train horses. Our horses would be like diamonds. He would carve them. I'd polish.

We found a place on the river about thirty miles from Billings. A trailer, small indoor arena, and some irrigated pasture. The banks turned us down for financing and Dick didn't even bother to ask his father—the Rooster was dead set against the horse trade—too romantic—so he asked Grandpa Alistair. That took courage.

Dick never said much when he came back. He sat at the kitchen table a while, and I just waited. Finally he said, "Grandpa doesn't think much of the horse business either.

"But he said he would help us get started with some sheep," he added.

He paused for a moment, staring down at his boots, then he said, "Marci, I can't do it. For the life of me I can't be a sheepherder."

I smiled and told him that was OK. I understood. We would get our dream some other way. I was amazed Alistair had offered to help at all. So we hit the road in pursuit of our dream.

We've been drifting ever since. Fourteen years of bouncing around from one cow camp to another, living in shacks, barns, mobile homes; never owning more that we can get in the back of a pickup. I have viewed life through the cracked windshield of our old pickup; cleaned more dirty little cowcamp shacks than I can count. Just following Dick and his dream. At first it was fun. We were young and in love and sang along with the radio. We rodeoed on weekends. Bullet-proof, Dick called us. Loose as ashes in the wind. "Buried treasure awaits us," he used to laugh. "We are destined for it."

When things got really tough, Dick went back to work for his father.

To be honest, I detested the Rooster. He was a rude, arrogant little man who wanted to be the legend his father was. If Dick wasn't up by four, he'd walk right into our bedroom and shake him awake. I hated it. Dick and I fought more and Dick and the Rooster fought constantly. But it never lasted long. Five, six, seven months and Dick would leave in a huff.

I had a father who gave me everything. The Rooster gave nothing except a reason to hit the road. I have seen the West, that's for sure. Wyoming, South Dakota, Nebraska, Nevada, Utah, Colorado, Idaho, Oregon, and British Columbia. Always looking for Dick's perfect place: a little ranch with good grass and water and an elderly couple with no children. Dick joked that they'd adopt us because of our ambition and honesty. After a while, he seemed serious and I realized he wasn't just in search of land. He wanted a mother and father.

I hardly knew his mother. Her name was Sarah. She was gentle and sweet but plumb wore out. Warren leaving home tore her heart out and she had little left to give Dick. He resented her weakness and seldom talked of her.

He never talked about Warren much either. One night in Idaho, after a barroom bet, half the town followed us to a gym where Dick dunked a basketball with his boots on. He could leap like a cat. That night in bed I asked him why he did it, other than money.

"My way of answerin' Warren's letters," he said. And that's all he said. Talking to me has never been one of Dick's strong points. At least, he doesn't talk about anything that matters.

What he does talk about are his dreams: the perfect ranch miles from anywhere. His own little kingdom with borders wide enough to keep everyone out.

Me, I want the Kingdom of God. But Dick won't talk about religion. Said he gave his word to Grandpa Alistair, then he laughs. I hit the bottom in Scottsbluff, Nebraska, two years ago. I called Reba in the middle of the night, and she led me to Jesus over the phone. It took me almost a year to share my conversion with Dick.

"So you got religion?" he said. "Don't worry. It's like mud on your boots. It'll wear off after a while."

He does his best to wear it off. There have been no dreams. No perfect ranches. No kingdoms. Just slave work. All the jobs are about the same. The rich bosses are selfish and demanding, the poor ones mean and drunk. All of them seem to ask something of Dick that he won't do.

One wanted me to cook for a crew of twenty men at no extra salary. Dick would have none of that. He didn't mind me working, but he expected me to be paid.

It's best when a boss lets me ride too. But most won't. When one said no, Dick just laughed and said, "You couldn't afford her anyway."

In Utah we went to work for a nice Mormon family. But to stay on we had to go to their church. Dick had the truck packed so fast that I'm still missing silverware.

Dick says religion is for hypocrites, weaklings, and old women. "Rodeos are better for meeting women," he says. His religion is blue sky, hard work, and cowboy pride. In other words, he worships himself.

I'm not saying Dick is a bad person. He's not. I mean, he sometimes does bad things but with good intentions.

One rancher wanted Dick to guide hunters during the fall. Dick loves wildlife and doesn't hunt. One day three Pennsylvania hunters killed a big buck just for the antlers. They planned on leaving the meat to rot.

"Gut that deer out," Dick told them.

They didn't want to.

So Dick field-dressed the deer, took the heart, cut it in three pieces and gave one to each hunter. "Eat what you kill," he said.

One of them said: "This will cost you your job, cowboy."

And Dick is supposed to have said: "It'll be worth it. Ain't much of a job anyway."

Then "the look" probably came over him. It's a half-crazed, willful stare that boils up from the bottom of his stomach and beams out of his eyes like lasers. It makes him look like Grandpa Alistair.

They ate it raw. That's what the boss said when he fired us.

I asked Dick about it as we drove away and he said: "Now, Marci, do you really think I could make three grown men with rifles eat raw meat?"

"Yes. Yes, I do," I told him. "I've seen you look at me like that."

"When?"

"The abortion," I said.

Dick doesn't want children. He wants ideals. Dreams. He wants to walk down a street and have everyone think he is a man of principles. Well, he is that, and he's proved it enough.

Like the time in Nevada. He was on a buckaroo outfit in the desert. A roundup wagon and ten men. I was stuck twenty minutes away at a dirty little cowcamp that had Playboy calendars on the walls—until I took them down.

Cowboys and buckaroos do the same work but they aren't the same breed. The northern cowboy doesn't draw attention to himself—Dick says that's because they all started as horse thieves. Buckaroos like silver-mounted bits, Spanish spurs, chinks, big floppy hats, and pants tucked into colorful high-topped boots. Gypsy stuff. In his old Levi jacket and shotgun chaps, Dick looked like a Republican among Democrats.

Anyway, on this particular wagon there was a horsebeater. The man was a rep; he didn't work for the outfit. He worked for a neighboring ranch. Dick hated to see that horse get beat but there wasn't much he could do. It wasn't his horse. So he bought it.

"I gave fifteen hundred for him," Dick told me. He said it like he wasn't proud or ashamed, it was just a fact. That was a lot of money then—three months' wages—and one good eyeful could tell you the bay was only a thousand dollar horse at best.

The foreman told Dick that it was against ranch policy to ride private stock. But he said they would buy the bay. For $800.

"Can you swear that the horsebeater will never own him again?" Dick asked.

The foreman said he couldn't guarantee that.

So Dick quit. He gave the horse to an old broken-down bullrider outside of Elko.

We worked there two months for a thousand dollars, so we left five hundred in the hole. But that's the way Dick is. A firm believer in the code of the West.

Cowboys are like monks or priests. They take vows of poverty. I wish they'd take a vow of celibacy instead.

But they believe in their word. Dick says a man's word is all he takes with him to the grave and there's nothing after that.

He thinks by being godless he can be guiltless. But I know differently. I am there in the night when he has nightmares about the black man. The African-American, I mean.

Dick's a joker, but he isn't racist. At least, not when he's one-on-one with a black or an Indian. But if he's out drinking with the boys, then he's less than whole.

He has a lot of buried guilt about that joke on the black man. It festers inside of him like a cocklebur in his soul.

One time we were traveling across this barren stretch of eastern Wyoming, just miles and miles of cactus, sage, and thistle. It was twilight and we were going to a new job and neither of us had talked for an hour. All of a sudden Dick said: "You know, my best friend in Nam was black." That was all he said. I nodded, and we kept on driving. I thought he might say more but I didn't really expect him to. And I sure didn't push it. The land about us was like an extension of Dick's soul. The prairie was flat and dry and dotted with scrub brush, and as we glided through it, it rolled up behind us as if it was some gigantic scroll.

I went to Marci as soon as her story drifted away. I was ashamed of my ambivalence toward her. Of all people, I should have empathy for a Christian woman married to a McColley.

"I'm sorry for seeming to avoid you," I told her. "But Donald likes having me near when he is under pressure."

"Is he worried about the speech?" Marci asked.

"Yes," I said. "But he'll be fine. Now then, tell me about you. How are you doing?"

She was cool and direct. Her earlier exuberance had been a desperate attempt at optimism. She was fading. The Andrew Murray book was closed and put away. "I'm miserable, Reba," she said.

"Tell me."

"Isn't that a terrible thing to say? I am a Christian. I should be happy. But I'm miserable. Or should I say one part of me is miserable, and one part is doing great? Doesn't that sound wonderful? I'm going schizo."

"I've been there," I said.

"My marriage is the pits."

"I'm sorry . . ."

"Reba, I used to get upset with Dick because of beard stubble in the sink and leaving the toilet lid up; for not keeping a job more than six months. None of that matters to me now. I want to share a Bible study with him." Tears were squeezing from the corners of her blue eyes. She dabbed them away self-consciously.

"That is an alien world to Dick," I said. "It might as well be another planet. Grandpa Alistair raised his offspring to be atheists and agnostics. It's all they know."

"Sometimes I think I was happier before I came to the Lord," she said.

"Marci, do you remember your call from Nebraska?"

She pursed her lips which made her chin lift and dimple. Her head gave a sad nod.

"You two were out of work, out of money, and Dick was drunk in a bar. Things can't be any worse now, can they?"

"I didn't know how miserable I was then," she said. "Now I know. Reba, believe me, some days I think I'm going crazy. I try to tell Dick, and he either blames religion or PMS."

"He lost his father only a year ago. I'm sure he is still hurting deeply."

"He's hurting? I'm hurting. I think I'm going nuts."

"Marci, I had a nervous breakdown three years after I married Donald. I know what you are going through."

"You?" The shock could have been carved from her face and laid on the table.

"Yes, me." I smiled, "I know, you thought I was spiritually perfect."

"No, but . . ."

"I know what you are going through," I said again. "And I know the Lord will see you through it. Let me give you one key. Love and honor your husband. I know it will be hard. He will seem very unlovable at times. But respect him anyway. Men want respect more than anything else. Their whole world is built around it. That's why we are here tonight at a banquet for Alistair. The world, as he knew it, is showing him respect."

"But he was a mean, selfish little man," Marci said. "He buried all of his money instead of sharing it, and he even killed a man."

"He was tough, shrewd, and proud," I said. "The world honors those traits."

"Well, I won't be seeing him in heaven, " she said. "I'm sure of that."

"Marci, we can never be sure of that."

"Maybe. I don't know. I just want Dick in heaven. But Dick's idea of heaven is his own place here on earth. A ranch where no one can bother him. Land. That's all Dick wants."

"I know," I said. "Land is the great definer and the great divider of the McColley soul."

"Land is only a part of it. Why are men so afraid of spiritual things?" She gulped from her water glass as if to quench her inner dryness.

"They are afraid of being deceived," I said.

"I think they are afraid of themselves."

I could not argue with that.

Marci brought her glass back to her lips. It was empty. "He doesn't talk anymore. Unless it's weather, horses, cattle, or land. That's all he ever talks about."

"That's all he ever did talk about, Marci. That's who he is."

"Reba, I hate to say this, but I don't like who he is."

"Marci, don't try to change him. That's God's job. The only person we are responsible for changing is ourselves."

"Well, all I know is, it's a terrible thing to be in love with a McColley." She stared across the room at the back of her broad-shouldered husband leaning against the bar.

I wanted to tell her I agreed. Nothing was harder than being in love with a McColley. But a voice inside stopped me.

Clara!

I turned. Clara was sitting alone at the table behind us. Her head was down. She seemed wrapped in herself. But I heard her screaming. She was screaming at me.

I heard Clara cry: *"Yes, there is! Yes, there is something harder than being in love with a McColley. The hardest thing of all is to be a McColley in love."*

6
Breakin' Ice

I just ain't in the mood for this. Would rather not be here at all. Everyone looks at me with tombstones in their eyes like they're lookin' at a ghost. I ain't the ghost. My pa is.

I know some are givin' me curious looks because of Pete. Pretty bold thing, me bringin' *him*, that's what they're thinkin'. I saw my cousin Warren studyin' us and could tell he was tryin' to figure out what the deal was, whether we were married or not. Same goes for Reba and Marci. Just because they got husbands . . .

I hate this. I hate sittin' here thinkin' that at any moment my pa, Duncan McColley, could walk in actin' like he was just a little late for the party. Then he'd see Pete and there would be trouble, and Grandpa's big party would be ruined because I brought him.

I know it ain't so. I know Pa's dead, but until there's actually a funeral he'll never be buried in my mind.

None of this is botherin' my brother, Donald, the way it's botherin' me, but why should it? He didn't live alone with Pa for the last twenty years. Besides, he thinks he's big stuff because he's givin' a speech tonight. One thing about Donald, he's always thinkin' about himself.

A memorial service I can understand—most of us didn't get to Grandpa Alistair's funeral 'cuz we were out lookin' for my pa, but electin' him to the Pioneer Hall of Fame? I don't savvy that. He was sure enough a pioneer, but he wasn't cut from the cloth that gets honors. Especially after killin' poor Mr. Hannson—which everyone knows was murder but no one will admit it.

Good grief, I just get the shakes sometimes. I get the chills like I was back on that pond the day Pa disappeared. What really chills me is knowin' the weather has warmed up, the snow is meltin' off, and somewhere out there a body will be uncovered.

I won't ever forget that day, or how cold I was.

We were breakin' ice down at the Slocum reservoir where it fills outa Swanny Creek. Pa, he always had to handle the ax. He'd chop till he got all red in the face, then he would stand back and sweat would freeze on his brow while I scooped the ice chunks outa the holes.

We only had a hundred and twenty cows waterin' there then, but he'd make sure he cut four good holes a day. Sometimes that ice was nearly a foot thick. I remember my cousin, Dick, tellin' me once that his pa, my uncle Roland, never would do the ice choppin'. He made Dick do it. That wasn't the way with Pa. He cut his own holes.

Good grief, it was cold that day. There was a raw wind blowin' outa the east—Pa always said the east wind was the worst—and no way could you face it. You just had to turn your back and kinda hunker down into yourself. It was January. January fourth.

From where I was standin' then, I could look down Swanny Creek and see the power pole standin' straight and dark against fields of snow. There's an electric well down there, a good one too. There was never no need for us to be choppin' ice. All we had to do was go down and turn the well on, and we'd have all the runnin' water we'd ever want. But Pa, he'd never do that. Too much trouble, he thought. Used too much electricity. He said the mice was always electrocutin' themselves chewin' on the wires in the well-house, then the whole shebang would short out and the well would freeze up.

The well-house is just a culvert with a lid on it that sits down in the ground about six feet. Inside there's a pressure tank and some valves, an electrical outlet, and assorted wires. Mice and snakes and things were always gettin' in there and becoming crispy critters. "Just a good place for things to die," Pa always said, like the worst mistake he ever made in his life was havin' that well drilled.

Ma talked him into it. That was twenty-one years ago, the winter before she died. He used it that first winter. But after the diabetes finally claimed Ma, he turned the well off. It was like the well represented her grave or somethin'. Mostly he was just cheap. The well meant usin' electricity, and he hated givin' the Rural Electric Co-op any more money.

I stayed to help Pa the past sixteen years. I cooked the meals, did the dishes, fixed fences, put up hay, and did most of the cow work. Never was put on a wage. Oh, he gave me a little spendin' money now and then but not much. He was afraid I would go to town and spend it. Heck, our place is one of the most remote in the country. It's forty-nine miles to Yellow Rock and thirty-seven miles to the little town of Hell's Bend, gravel road all the way to either one. The main thing, of course, was that he wanted to keep me out of town so I couldn't see *him*. He could never call him Pete, or even That Andraxie Fellow, it was always *him*, like he had a sex but no real personality.

After breakin' ice that day on the Slocum pond, we got in the pickup and headed home. Weatherman kept issuin' stockmen's warnings. Pa was a great one for always listenin' to the radio. Dick said his dad was even worse. Some people like seclusion but can't stand silence. At home I fixed lunch while he sat in his old tattered rocker and listened to the radio some more. We had ham sandwiches and split-pea soup, and he said he was worried about that little bunch of cows that was missin'. The weatherman said there was a real Arctic blast movin' in, lots of wind and snow.

Our place is laid out like a long rectangle. On one end is our house and the Slocum pond. Running right through the middle of the place, lengthwise, is a rough divide. Badlands. Below that divide is a little flat area and that's where the ranch ends. Now there ain't any real grass or water in those badlands, but there is shelter and sometimes the cows blow down in there, then they get too lazy to turn around and walk back out. A four-wheel drive can make it, but it's slow goin'.

Pa figured those twenty head of missin' cows was down in the roughs, and he wanted to get them out before a big snow socked 'em in for good. I told him I'd go with him but he wouldn't hear of it. "What dang sense does that make?" he snapped at me. "Then if somethin' happens we'd both be stuck down there."

I didn't argue. If there was one thing in life I learned, it was that you didn't argue with Pa. Only Grandpa Alistair was allowed to do that.

That was a real curious afternoon. After Pa left, the house seemed real lonely. Usually I relished him being gone. I left Tippy in—she's my little three-legged border collie. She lost one foot in a coyote trap years ago—and I made her stay on the rug by the door. I thought about callin' Pete. Figured I could reach him at the Hellroarin' Bar in Hell's Bend, but I hated callin' collect and Pa was always checkin' the phone bill for clues to my sins. We'd only had a phone for fifteen years, and he still wasn't used to it. He held the receiver out about a foot from his mouth and yelled at it. He yelled so loud he didn't even need the phone. You could hear him clear to Yellow Rock.

I wandered about the house a bit but couldn't find nothing to do. I tried reading a novel that was overdue from the library, but it wouldn't hold my interest. All these rural areas have historical books of some sort, and

I picked up one of those and thumbed through it. It's filled with stories and photos of pioneers and their families. Mostly it's pictures of people standin' in front of tarpaper shacks. The men are lean and hard lookin', and the women look tired and worn. There's usually a pole corral and a skinny horse in the background or a barn wall with coyote pelts tacked all over it. Sometimes the stories and photos are interestin', but other times, like that day, they just depress me because I realize how little things have changed.

I did look at our family photo. Grandpa Alistair as a young man. Fit and strong, already bald. Not any taller than the sad-lookin' woman standin' beside him. She looked like the shock of homesteadin' life had finally hit her. Two little boys in raggedy clothes. Uncle Roland and Pa. Two little babies in dresses sat in the dirt. Isabelle and Maybelle. The twins that died of the flu. I'd never noticed it before—and I'd looked at the picture many times wonderin' who I was by what I had come from—but Grandpa Alistair had a shovel in his hand. That unsettled me, and I put the book away.

Then I did the oddest thing. I went to Pa's room. I never went in there. He kept it real neat—said he learned to keep a place clean by livin' in a sheepwagon. I ran my hand across the bureau, and there was just a little bit of dust on it. There was a picture of my ma on the dresser and another picture of us kids and Ma and Pa. It was at some sort of community picnic. I was about six years old. Donald had just married Reba, she was barely visible in the background.

Then I went to my little room and just stood there for awhile listenin' to the wind begin to howl and feelin' the cold come through the cracks. It was like somethin' had a grip on me and I didn't know what it was. Then I turned and saw myself in my full-length mirror by my bed. Slowly I unbuttoned my blouse and took it off, then just stood there in that chilly room, starin' at myself in the mirror.

Look at you, I told myself, there you are, thirty-five years old and wastin' your life away. Ain't got a husband. Ain't got any kids. Ain't got any money. I reached up and let my hair down, then stood sideways and inspected myself. Gettin' gray, I told myself, and look at those wrinkles. Cold and wind and sun, it sure ages a woman. I patted my stomach. It was still lean and hard like a teenage boy's. Hard work had done that. Hard work and no babies. I ran my hands down my arms and was embarrassed by the muscles. A woman shouldn't look like that. I was cold. Goosebumps were risin' on my big, masculine arms so I put my blouse back on and slipped a sweater over it. Then I went back out to the living room, turned on the radio, picked up a piece of rawhide braidin' I'd been workin' on, and waited for Pa.

By four-thirty it was pretty dark, and the wind was really beginning to rattle the windows. A good five inches of new snow had fallen from the time I sat down to my braidin' until I finally started to worry. Pa figured

strong flesh whipped any weather, but his old flesh
wasn't as strong as it used to be. Besides that, any
number of things can go wrong with a pickup in cold
weather.

I knew if anything serious happened I was supposed to call one of the neighbors, but I also knew
Pa would be madder than dickens if I called them out
on a false alarm. So that just left me one alternative.
I had to go look for him myself. I got all bundled up
and went outside and unplugged my old '72 GMC
pickup. It's just a two-wheel drive half-ton, but I keep
about four hundred pounds of sacked feed in the
back for traction. I knew I couldn't make it down the
jeep trail into the badlands but I could drive the main
pasture roads.

It was pitch dark and the wind was whippin' the snow
in my headlights. The radio said it was thirty below with
a thirty-mile-an-hour wind. Pa would have called that a
thirty-thirty night and said somethin' like: "Might as well
put a .30-.30 to your head." I had to put chains on but
still got stuck twice. But I managed to shovel myself out.
We McColleys are handy with shovels.

I drove to where the jeep trail falls off into the
badlands and couldn't see any fresh tracks of any kind,
but the way the wind was driftin' the snow, that didn't
surprise me. I drove back to Slocum pond and down to
the well, then figured I'd better get back home. I figured
Pa would be there waitin' for me.

When I saw the house was dark my heart about fell
through my stomach. He was still out there somewhere.

I came in and tried the phone but it wasn't workin'. I learned later the wind had blowed the line down. I grabbed some blankets, a thermos of coffee, and two good flashlights and headed back out.

I drove back to the badlands and left my pickup sittin' at the top of the hill with the lights on and the motor running. Then I headed down the trail on foot, picking my way with the beam of a flashlight. It was terrible cold and dark. I tried yellin', but the wind just blew the words back into my mouth and frosted my lungs.

A mind plays on ya hard at a time like that. Part of me was sayin' that he probably got stuck but he had the good sense to just sit in the truck and wait the storm out. Another part of me realized he'd try shovelin' himself out and might have had a stroke or somethin'.

The further I walked I thought maybe I was lost. I couldn't make out any sign of bein' on a trail. I wished I'd brought Tippy. But what good is a three-legged dog in deep snow?

Visibility was so poor I almost bumped into his truck. It was sittin' pointed uphill, hood-deep in a big snowbank. The motor wasn't runnin' which scared me at first, then I thought, *No, that's good because if the motor was runnin' he probably got gassed to death by the exhaust.*

I opened the door hopin' to see him but he wasn't there. For the first time I really was worried. Sick to my stomach worried. I climbed back outa there and got to my truck. I drove the pasture roads again. Once I thought I saw him, somethin' standin' dark and thin at the edge of my headlights. But it was just a powerpole.

I was back at the well below the Slocum pond. I kept gettin' stuck and each time it was harder to shovel myself out. Finally I knew I had to get back to the house. There wasn't anything I could do but wait. Maybe the old man had crawled into a washout or cave and was just waitin' the storm out in the badlands. That would be about like him. Everyone said he was part coyote.

That was a terrible night. I hardly slept a-tall. When I did nod off it was just for a few minutes and then it was daylight. The storm was over and the sky was blue and quiet. The snow was fresh and white and the temperature was thirty-eight below. I managed to make it to the county road and down to a neighbor's. Their phone was workin' so we called all the other neighbors. It wasn't no time till they was showin' up in pickups and snowmobiles and a couple of them even had planes.

We searched all day long and much of the night. The County Search and Rescue Team came out. They had a plane, three snowmobiles and dogs. The neighbor ladies kept everybody fed, they filled our little kitchen with hot meals, but I didn't eat. Pete came out as soon as he heard. He was the only one who saddled up and went lookin' horseback.

After the second full day I knew there wasn't any hope. I could see it in the faces of my neighbors. They all told me they would stay and look as long as I wanted them to, but I knew it was foolish. They all had cows to feed and kids to take care of, and wherever the old man was it wasn't going to make any difference now. The women loaded up their empty pans but made sure my refrigerator and cupboards were stocked. They all hugged me before they left and told me to be strong.

When they were all gone Pete was still there. He stood at the door lookin' at me as if I was supposed to tell him if he should leave or stay. I didn't say anything at all so he stayed. I needed his help. I had cows to feed. He went back to Hell's Bend to get his personal things.

The days dragged on and I was in a daze. I had called Donald as soon as I could, but he had to wait for the roads to clear. It's a long ways to Great Falls. He made it after the neighbors had left. Good thing Pete wasn't around at the time.

I'll find Pa, Donald insisted. He was out the better part of the day but gave up. He came back and strode about the house like he was takin' inventory.

"You know he probably doesn't have a will," he told me.

"Probably doesn't," I said.

"I'll take care of it," he said, and suddenly I didn't feel too secure. Hearin' Donald say he'd take care of it was like bein' invited to your own hangin'. Luckily he was gone by the time Pete got back from Hell's Bend. Pete's as easy-going as a fresh-suckled pup, but he doesn't hold no trust in my brother.

The day after Donald left, the co-op fixed the phone and I got a call tellin' me that Grandpa Allstair had passed away. "We been tryin' to reach you for three days," they said. Meanwhile, they had had a funeral without us.

I tried to piece it all together. Pa had disappeared on a Friday afternoon. Grandpa had died that day. Donald showed up Monday, Grandpa was buried on Tuesday, and I got the call about him that night. Lord, what a week that was.

As bad as the daytime hours were, the nights were worse. Every night I dreamed about finding Pa. Sometimes I was in my pickup drivin' through the hills, and I would look over and see a hand stickin' out of a snowbank. Other times I would dream that I was awakened by a noise outside and I would get up and turn on the porchlight, and there was Tippy chewin' on somethin' she'd drug down outa the hills. A piece of Pa.

At first Pete rolled a sleepin' bag out on the living room floor but eventually he was in my room. Then the dreams changed. I would dream I heard a noise and got up, and there was Pa sittin' in his old tattered rocker, rockin' away and he would look at me accusingly and say: "You're sleepin' with *him*, ain't you?" I knew I shouldn't be. Ma had taught me enough Bible to know that. So I told Pete and he just rolled his sleepin' bag out on the floor again.

I never knew why Pa hated him so much. Pete's older than I am, and it's true he's never been nothin' but a cowboy all his life, and some people say he's just a drunk, but he's a kind man at heart. And since the day Pa disappeared, I haven't seen him take a drink, not one.

We got married about the first day of February. I was hopin' it would make the dreams end. We went to a Justice of the Peace in Hell's Bend. At first we had a hard time findin' anyone who could do it, and Pete said, "I wonder if it's legal if a Brand Inspector does it?" I told him I didn't think so.

The dreams have been weakenin' since then, but reality is still the same. Some days I'm real happy. I have a good husband, and we have nice little place in the country. But the fact is there is still a body out there somewhere, and we don't even know what the legal situation is. I think it's seven years before a missin' person is declared dead. Then there's the matter of the will. I'm sure Donald's right about Pa not havin' one. The lawyer in Yellow Rock said we might be up the creek and asked if we had any paddles. I know us McColleys. Grandpa, Pa, Uncle Roland, Donald, Dick. They're all the same. They'd kill for land. Or water. That's what Grandpa did.

In some ways, it might be better if the body is never found. That way Pete and I might get at least seven years together on the place.

But I want him found. I want the dreams to end.

I could just make an announcement and let everyone know we're married. That might be enough to make Pa roll over in his grave and roll out to where he would be discovered.

But I don't want to do it here, not tonight. This is supposed to be Grandpa Alistair's night, and I don't want to take away from that.

But I will be just as glad when tonight is over and Pete and I can go home. Springtime is upon us. Soon the cows will start calvin'. The body will either be found or not be found. I know Pete plans on bein' horseback a lot. He wants to be the one that finds the body, not me. We both know it won't be a pretty sight.

Sometimes I wonder what Pete would do if he found it. I think he would want to do the right thing and bring it home and give it a proper burial. He's that type of man. But, without there bein' a will and all, I ain't sayin' that either one of us might not be tempted to do a little buryin' of our own. Oh, God, that's a terrible thing to say, isn't it?

I know that there's a couple of things that can be done if I have the power to do 'em. I'm gonna sell that little jag of bunch-quittin' cows that kept goin' down under the divide. They could put the money in escrow or a trust or whatever, but I want those cows gone.

Then if Pete and I are still on the place next winter, the first thing we are gonna do is use that well. No more breakin' ice in the freezin' cold. The first real day of winter next year I am gonna go down, crawl in that well-house, and turn the valves on.

Let the water flow, that's the way I see it.

A cold, white pond coated with virgin snow and a stark, upright powerpole standing in the distance. This vision was retreating from my mind and people's faces slowly emerged from the field of snow and I could hear my name, repeated like an echo, as the banquet again took focus.

"Reba. Reba." It was Marci.

"What?"

"You seem totally spaced out. Are you OK?"

"I'm fine, I think."

"I don't think you heard a word I said," Marci scolded me.

"I'm sorry. What were you saying?"

"I was telling you what a terrible Christian I am."

"Oh, Marci, you're not—"

"Yes, I am. Here I sit feeling sorry for myself when the one who really has it tough is Clara. We need to go talk to her."

"Uh, Clara?"

"Yes, come on."

The banquet hall was slowly filling. I glanced at Donald to see if he was missing me. Marci was already sitting beside Clara, who looked up with the startled, glassy eyes of a deer caught in the headlights of a car. I saw her slim shoulders stiffen as I seated myself.

"Clara," Marci said, "I'm so sorry about your father and I'm sorry we didn't come help search. But we didn't even know about it."

"That's OK, Marci," Clara said. "We had lots of help and it didn't do any good."

"Who knows?" Marci said. "Maybe he hurt his head and . . ."

"And what?" Clara said. "Wandered to a town where he got on a bus and disappeared? Marci, it's thirty-five miles to Yellow Rock from the ranch, and it was in the middle of a blizzard."

"I know," Marci said, "but—"

"But there's no body. I know. I know you are tryin' to give me hope, but there isn't anything I haven't thought of. I have stayed up many a night thinking of every possible place he could be. He's out there somewhere and he is dead."

Marci sighed. "I know you are probably right. Old-time ranchers don't just up and leave their place."

"Pa hadn't left the ranch for thirty years, besides goin' to Yellow Rock or Hell's Bend. And the bull sales in Glasgow," Clara said. "He had no place he wanted to go, except Scotland, and he knew he'd never do that."

"He wanted to go to Scotland?" I asked.

"Oh, it was just a dream of his. He wanted to see the land where ol' Alistair was born. Grandpa and my pa hardly ever talked, but I still think Pa worshipped him. But he knew there was only one chance that the dream could ever come true."

"What was that?" Marci asked.

Clara looked at her dubiously. "Well, if he found Grandpa's buried gold, of course."

"What gold?" Marci asked.

Clara laughed. "You're a McColley and you don't know. Dickie never told you?"

"He's talked about buried treasure," Marci said. "I thought it was just a saying, a figure of speech."

"It could be," I said. "No one knows if there is any gold."

"Pa thought so," Clara said, "and I bet he was still lookin' for it up until he"—she shuddered—"until, until whatever happened. He froze, I suppose."

"Perhaps we should change the subject," I suggested.

"Things will work out," Marci said. "That's Romans 8:28, isn't it, Reba? All things work out good in the end."

To those who love God and are called according to His purpose, I wanted to say.

"Things are already workin' out," Clara said, and she stared out at the bar where Pete and Dick were still talking.

"Oh," Marci said, "I suppose they are."

"I know you two mean well, comin' to cheer me up and all," Clara said. "But no, Reba, I ain't got around to readin' the books you sent me. I haven't read anything religious since my mother died. And I have to admit I have always been jealous of both of you."

"Jealous? Of us?" Marci asked.

"Sure. You're both so pretty. Marci the rodeo queen. Me, I sit a horse like a sack of potatoes. And Reba's got children and even grandchildren. I guess I don't envy either one of you for the husbands you've got. I can't imagine bein' married to my brother, and Dickie, he's just a feather blowin' in the wind."

I thought Marci was going to become angry. But she surprised me. She took Clara's hand. "Clara," she said, "you are very pretty. I have always thought so."

"Me?" Clara said. "You gotta be kidding."

"No," Marci said. "You are very attractive."

Clara blushed. "Well, thanks, but it don't really make any difference now."

"And just so you will know," Marci said. "I will never be the one for judging you for loving Pete Andraxie."

Clara's eyes softened and rimmed with tears. "He's the only man I've ever loved," she said sternly.

"I'm sure it hasn't been easy," Marci said.

Clara shrugged. "That's the way it is, ain't it? We love the men we love and pay the price as we go."

Marci reached out and put an arm around Clara's shoulders. Clara allowed it. I felt eyes on me. Eyes that seemed to open my mind like a surgical whisper. Soft, curious, questioning eyes. I let my head be pulled by the gaze. A man was standing, leaning with one elbow against the bar, staring at me. *Well, hello, Pete Andraxie,* I said to myself.

"Hello yourself," I heard him say.

7
Tremors

I have known the McColleys all my life. If I was a speechmaker I'd be the one to give the speech. I ain't sayin' they are evil people, but I guess they have caused their share of misery. I was nineteen when old Alistair cut down the Big Swede with one swoop of a shovel. I don't know if it was murder or not. The jury didn't think so.

My father was a ranchhand, he never owned a place of his own and had nothin' to leave his four boys when he departed this life. Two of the ranches he worked for bordered ol' Alistair, another bordered Duncan's place.

I was still in diapers when I first crossed paths with them. We got to know most of our neighbors by helpin' at brandin's. My old man was always one to be helpin' others. He thought brandin's were a big party. Lots of hard work, good food, visitin', and beer. He always drug us boys along to be part of the crew. By the time I was four, I was a horseback for the gatherin' and packin' the nut-bucket durin' the ground work. As we got bigger we did more physical work, like wrestlin' calves.

The old man let us drink beer. Especially me for some reason. He'd throw me a cold one from the cooler and yell, "Put a church key to this one, Petey-boy." That was before pop-tops, when everyone called a can opener a church key.

I learned to like the cold foam and malty taste. At first I pretended to get drunk, and the men laughed and urged me on. Soon I was getting drunk for real. The adults liked it and I liked being liked. How old was I then? Probably six or seven. It wasn't long before I couldn't even drink pop. It was too sweet. Beer was all I wanted.

One brandin' was especially hot and the beer made me sick. I staggered around, ready to throw up, and just outside my swirl of sickness I could hear the men laughin'. The laughter pounded against me like waves on a bank. I was about to crumble. Then someone led me away and layed me down in the shade of the corrals in soft, green grass. A soft voice soothed me. I thought it was an angel talkin' to me, but as I fell asleep I knew it was someone prayin'. I layed real still and listened. I'd never heard anyone talk to God before. Warm hands were laid on my forehead, and peace rocked me to sleep.

Later my old man got really sore. He said I'd disgraced him for sleepin' through work. The whole next week he cursed the woman who had led me away. Martha McColley, Clara's mother.

I dropped outa school when I was sixteen and went to work on a ranch. There were four of us cowboys out in a line-shack. We drank everyday but we got our work done. Not one of us ever missed a day of work in three years. Then I got to driftin'. Workin' here and there.

I saw all the McColley kids grow up, even Donald, who was six years older than me. He was a bully until the rest of us outgrew him, which didn't take too long. Dick was wild as a wet cat, but a good little hand. Nothin' scared him. Warren was always off by himself, studyin' the rest of us from a distance like he didn't approve of what he was seein'. Clara was special. One moment she was wrestlin' calves with the rest of us, and the next moment she was pickin' wildflowers and puttin' 'em in her hair. She just had country written all over her.

My thinking that Clara was special intensified when she was about sixteen. I was twenty-six. Her pa was sure sour about her being around an older man. Especially one who drank. He threw around enough threats that we started seein' each other on the sly.

By the next year, my love for Clara had me wantin' to quit the bottle. I learned that there were a lot of good, respectable people around and I wasn't one of 'em. I'd never been invited to someone's house for dinner or sat next to someone in church. All I'd known were cow-camps and bars.

One night Clara and I were out on the prairie, and I was tellin' her how much I loved the cowboy life, the fresh air and sunsets, the wild critters and open spaces. I told her I loved the sound of the wind rustlin' through the trees and the crunch of horses' hooves on fresh-fallen leaves.

She looked at me and said: "If you love all of that so much, how come you spend so much time in those dark, dirty, foul-smellin' barrooms?"

I couldn't answer that. I knew cowboys who didn't drink. Some were even good family men who went to church. It didn't make them any less of a hand. That night I went back to my room at the Hellroarin' Hotel and told the manager to lock me in my room.

"Lock me up," I said. "And don't let me out or anyone in—no matter how much I scream—until three days have gone by."

"Ah, you'll starve or break the door down," he said.

"No, I won't," I said. "And I will pay for any damage I do." I didn't know about treatment centers. I was gonna quit the bottle on my own. There was a sink and a toilet in the room, and I had a loaf of bread. I figured that's all I needed.

Was it a hell on earth? I reckon it was. What I can remember anyway.

I expected a rough ride, but the bottle bucked a lot harder than I ever would have thought. The first night I ate all the bread, shaved three or four times, polished my boots, anything to keep busy. By mornin' I was gettin' hot and cold flashes. I spent the day pacin' the room. To the bed, to the wash basin, past the old rickety chair. There was no window in the room or I would have jumped out. I tried the door a thousand times. It was a good door. Solid wood with a black enamel knob.

The shakes got bad, and my skin started crawlin' the second night. I scratched myself raw from the itchin' and began shoutin' to be let out. I'd never known fear like that before. It got me to poundin' on the door, the walls, and the floor. There was only one other guest in the hotel, and he checked out that night.

I lost track of time. I ripped all my clothes off and never knew I'd done it. I think I secretly thought I could bust outa that place, but this was one of those good old hotels, the kind made by craftsmen. The walls were brick. I busted all the knuckles on my right hand, and it swelled up as big as a head and took on a mouth that began talkin' to me. That head chased me all around the room until I fell on the bed and covered it with pillows. I smothered it.

Sweat was runnin' down my face and I was freezin', and I looked down at the floor and there were snakes crawlin' outa my boots. Hundreds of 'em. I ain't never been afraid of snakes, but I was afraid of these. I pulled into a ball in the corner and screamed and cried, and then the spiders started fallin' from the ceiling. Big, ugly ones that crawled into my eyes and ears. I beat on 'em and whipped 'em with pillows, but they just kept comin'. 'Bout this time the boys down in the bar stepped out into the street to listen. You could hear me all over the little town of Hell's Bend. I was yellin' for help, yellin' for God, yellin' for Clara.

I swore to God I would never drink again if he would just get rid of the snakes and spiders. I was covered with sweat, blood, and vomit, but I didn't even know it. I didn't care about my body. I only cared about my mind. I was afraid I would never get it back, that I was outside the limits of time and self-control. All this had gone on for so long there wasn't even time anymore. Time had just quit and when time quits life becomes endless.

"God," I screamed. "Help me and I'll never drink again." And I heard Him. He told me to lay real still. I felt safe. I could feel a hand on my forehead. Suddenly I was that little boy again layin' in the green grass behind the corral, and Martha McColley became Clara, and she had her hands on me and was prayin': "Lord, save this boy from hell."

I felt like I had been hangin' from a rope but the rope was cut. I was driftin' free. I had whipped it. The terrible fever was breakin', and I was gonna wash up free and clean on a grassy riverbank.

Then I felt the hands. "Lie real still," a voice said. Only it wasn't Martha. It wasn't Clara. It was a man's voice. I felt somethin' smooth at my lips and the bite of a thousand wildcats on my tongue.

"No," I yelled. "Take it away! Take it away!"

"Lie real still, " the voice said.

I pushed but he pinned my arms to my side. The room was dark and my vision was bad but I could make out the form of a small, bald-headed man standin' above me.

He forced the bottle to my mouth. The whiskey splashed and spilled its way down my throat, explodin' like fire in my guts.

"No! Clara! Clara!"

A torrent of foul and muddy water washed me from the grassy bank, I was spinnin', sinkin', drownin' in filth. The dirty water filled my lungs, my stomach, my ears and eyes. I was drownin' without dyin'.

I passed out. It was many hours before I came to. I wasn't even half the man I was before. I was less. Somethin' inside me had died. I was less than a man, a boy, a slave chained to a post, naked, bleedin', and whipped.

I had whipped it. I had rode the drink demon to a stop. But someone had interfered. I didn't get a fair ride, but no one would know. I had failed, and Clara would never be mine.

I did not want to kill Duncan McColley. But I surely wanted to watch him die.

I never saw his face that night, just the outline of a small man with a round, bald head. But I felt his hands.

I tiptoed back to nothingness. I acted like I had never been gone. My friends had expected worse. They embraced my failure as a foregone conclusion. I drank more. I drank until there was nothin' to hear, nothin' to see, nothin' to remember.

I still saw Clara when she would see me, which was about one day a month when I managed to sober up.

I never asked the hotel manager how Duncan got in. It didn't make any difference.

I just accepted my fate.

"Reba, what in the world is going on?"

I was still in a sepia-toned hotel room with cold brick walls. A large man was writhin' on an iron-framed bed. I was nearly overcome with the Lord's compassion for the man.

I felt Marci's hand on my shoulder and looked into the warm concern of her blue eyes. "I'm having a strange night," I said.

"Join the crowd," Clara said.

Clara. I had forgotten about Clara.

"No, this is different," Marci said. "Something's wrong. Reba, are you feeling ill?"

"I didn't know," I said.

"You don't know? You've been shaking for the last ten minutes."

Shaking? Was I taking on the physical characteristics of the storytellers?

Clara gave me a suspicious look. She was becoming frightened. "I've seen someone shake like that before," she said.

"There is a strange spirit here tonight," Marci said.

I grimaced. I did not want Marci mentioning spirits.

"Well, excuse me," Clara said quietly, her eyes down, "but I really don't want to hear about strangeness. Besides, I have to go to the bathroom." She was running. I knew she would stay away as long as the conversation was spiritual.

Marci waited until Clara was out of earshot. "What is it, Reba? You're just not yourself."

"I think the Lord is moving in His mysterious ways," I said. I did want to talk to someone about the experiences, but I was wishing it was someone more spiritually mature than Marci. But who would that be?

Marci's lower lip made a subtle drop, and her eyes opened proportionately. "The Lord is showing you something, isn't He? I can feel it in the air."

"I do seem to be getting, uh, insights into people here," I said cautiously, panged by the guilt that Marci was one of the people.

"Words of knowledge?" she asked. "Are you being used prophetically?"

"I don't know," I said. I wondered how Marci knew so much.

"My church has been teaching on the gifts of the Spirit," she said. "Are you receiving revelation knowledge?"

"Maybe. I don't know. Probably not in the orthodox sense, anyway. To be honest, it's not real comfortable."

"Do you think it's satanic? Familiar spirits or something?"

"Marci, I don't know. I don't think it's anything like that." If it was demonic, the last thing I wanted was Marci stirring the cauldron.

"Have you gotten insights into me?"

I was in a spot. I didn't want to lie, but I didn't want to tell the truth either.

"You have, haven't you?"

"A little."

"Reba, do you know that I have been thinking about divorcing Dick?"

"No!"

"Well, I have."

"No, Marci, I haven't felt anything like that. Let's just say that I have felt your pain this evening, and your loneliness and frustrations."

"Well, I know God doesn't believe in divorce. But I need a break. I can't go on like this. I'm tired of living like a gypsy and being terrified to go to church or listen to Christian radio. I'm getting sick of country music and John Wayne movies—"

Marci was getting wound up. "Ah, excuse me," I said, "but I better touch base with Donald. He will be giving his speech pretty soon. We can talk about this later."

"What's the Lord showing you, Reba? Clara's father, do you know where he is?"

"Well—"

"What else?" she whispered. "Is there really missing gold? Do you know where it is? Not that I care. I really don't. Money doesn't mean anything to me anymore.

"Reba, is divorce really a sin? I mean, Dick hasn't cheated on me, but he made me kill our baby. I wasn't a Christian then, though. Can you write him somehow? Or maybe if you sent him some books. You send everyone books. You even sent Grandpa books."

"I'll pray about it," I said and realized how artificial that sounded.

"Reba, listen. If you are getting prophetic insights, maybe it is a call to intercession. Maybe we should sneak off somewhere and pray."

"That could be it," I said, rising from my chair. "But I better get back to Donald now." My heart was aching

with compassion for Marci, but I was walking a fine
boundary between spiritual kingdoms. I had to concentrate on my balance.

"Think about writing Dick," she said. "He might
listen to you."

"I have to go," I said. "Donald's speech."

Speech. I was hearing a speech.

A voice was beginning, but it wasn't Donald's. I
maneuvered through people, smiling superficially,
while drawn like a magnet to the chair by Donald's side.
He did not say anything, but I could tell he had been
waiting for me.

The voice was beginning. I softly put my hand on
Donald's arm. A tether to an anchor.

This voice was more natural, less intrusive.

It should have been. It was mine.

8
Speeches

Oh Donald, my Donald.

You labor so hard on what you hope will be immortal. They are serving the meal, so in moments you will be introduced to give your speech. I hope you don't embarrass yourself too greatly.

I think of Donald Junior and Donna, knowing you are disappointed that they are not here. You wish your only children could hear your speech. But the truth is, neither of those kids liked their great-grandfather. Alistair's gruff ways and foul language scared them as children, and as adults, they chose to ignore him as much as he had ignored them. And sadly, the same was true for their grandfather, Duncan. He has always been missing as far as they are concerned.

But what pains me most, my husband, is neither of the children feels close to you, either.

Take the cabin at the lake for example. The McColley
Mountain Mansion you call it. I heard Donna once call
it the McColley House of Misery. You labored for years
to buy that cabin. You ran the real estate business in
Great Falls and my father's farm. You worked the kids
so hard. As small children they spent countless hours
on tractors in the fields. For what? So you could have
a cabin at the lake. A place for the family, you said. Ten
years ago we got one. Three bedrooms on two acres
with a boathouse and dock.

Oh, Donald. The cabin became nothing more than
another project. You are the high priest of labor, a man
defined not by what he is, but by what he does.

And you do many things well and expect the same
from others. But no one can work with you. Not
Donald Junior. Not Donna. Certainly not me. We
spent all autumn at the cabin. You cut firewood, rebuilt
the dock, poured new sidewalks, put up swing sets.
"When is Donna coming with the kids?" you kept asking.

I kept telling you that Donna and the grandkids
weren't coming.

"When will Junior and Jean be here?"

"Junior and Jean can't get away," I said.

You began to get bitter. "I shouldn't have to be doing
all this myself," you said. "Where are the kids to help
me?"

I tried to help, but how much do I know about
concrete and two-by-fours? "Go get the plumb line!"
you screamed. I couldn't remember what a plumb line
was. "Get the level then!"

Where was it? Where was it? Oh, I didn't know. I tried to be patient with you. But I soon left you to your whirlwind of frenzy and retreated to the McColley sanctuary, the living room of the cabin, where I read the Bible and watched the storm clouds gather to the north.

We stayed longer than we should have. "Donald," I said. "If it snows we will be stuck here all winter. There's no way over the pass once it snows."

"It won't snow!" you snapped as if you controlled the elements. I remembered how I heard Donna calling you "God" to her friends. ("I can't go. God wants me to go to the cabin and work all weekend.") I wanted to correct her, tell her that it was blasphemy to equate you with God, but I didn't. Her definition of male authority is forever defined, carved in the heart you hardened. Only God Himself can soften it now.

When the snow began falling you still insisted staying an extra day. "Great Scott, Reba," you scolded, "I have to drain the pipes. You don't want all the pipes to burst, do you?"

Frankly, Donald, I did not care.

The next morning we packed the van, closed up the cabin for winter, and began the long, winding ascent up Tiberus Pass. I closed my eyes and pretended to sleep. But I was praying. It was very quiet in the van. I could hear the engine labor and felt the tire slipping in the search for traction.

"Did you bring the chains?" I asked. You didn't answer.

When I opened my eyes we were near the top of the pass, above timberline. Giant granite boulders sat at the road's edge like snow-capped toll-monsters. Wet snow-flakes the size of quarters exploded on the windshield. Everything was gray. We were inside a cloud. I realized we were not moving.

"What's wrong, Donald?"

"We've slid off the road," you said. "We're stuck."

"Did you bring the chains?"

You mumbled something that I took to be a no, pulled your collar up, put your gloves on, and stepped outside. I was instantly scared. As strong and as smart as you think you are, Donald, you are not as strong as a winter storm or miles of mountains. You dug with the portable shovel. You leaned and pushed against the back of the van. I heard the rear door open, and in my mirror I watched you drag out clothes and push them under the tires for traction.

I put on my stocking cap and gloves and joined you. We worked in silence. You got in and drove while I pushed against the van and rearranged the bed-spreads, shirts and slacks that were spinning out from beneath the wheels. I got so very cold. Finally I told you I had to warm up. We got back in the van and turned the heater on high. I poured us coffee from a thermos.

"What do we do next?" I asked.

You did not answer for a long time. It seemed to take minutes for your mind to clear of boat docks, firewood, concrete, Donna and the kids, Junior and Jean.

"If the van won't go forward," you said, "we will have to try to go backwards. We have to get back to the cabin and find the chains."

You jacked the back of the van up and we put everything we could under the tires. We did the same at the front. You told me to stand clear, and you climbed in. The engine roared, the van lurched backwards, crumpling suitcases and splintering the kitchen countertop you had promised to restore. You gestured wildly, and I ran down the slick blacktop, caught a door handle and pulled myself in. "I don't dare stop," you told me.

You began backing slowly off the mountaintop. I could feel you battle for the tender balance between braking and momentum, of traction and slippage. Your face was red and beaded with sweat, but your knuckles on the steering wheel were slowly turning blue and white. You looked older than fifty-one.

It's seven miles, I thought. Seven miles downhill at what? Four, five miles-an-hour? In a snowstorm.

"I can't see!" you shouted. It was true. The storm had suddenly intensified.

"Reba, there's a flashlight in the back. Get it. You will have to get out and guide me." I rummaged until I found it. "I can't stop," you said. "You will have to get out while the van's moving, then run and get behind it. No matter what you do, stay in the middle of the road and keep the flashlight pointed at my side mirror."

I stepped out into the gray cold. My feet slipped and I fell against the van. I was afraid I would fall under it, but I righted myself and ran. I could not see the highway nor the sides of the road. The wind and snow bit into my face and stung my eyes. I stomped my feet to feel hard smoothness. It felt like blacktop. I heard the quiet hum of the van's engine and a vague outline of its silver elephantine shape. I walked backwards, pointing the flashlight in front of me, guessing where the mirror would be. Seven miles!

I never suspected the sharp curve. There were no dimensions. I felt like I was adrift in space until something hard pressed into the backs of my legs. I started to fall backwards, but turned and caught myself hugging a boulder. The flashlight fell from my hands. I saw the light recede to nothingness. I could not hear a clatter when it hit. The van! I turned in terror. It was still coming.

"Donald! Stop! Stop!" I screamed.

You could not hear me, Donald.

At the last instant I fell to the side. The bumper hit the boulder. The van stopped, the left hind wheel only inches from my legs. You got out, and I heard you call my name.

"Here," I said.

You pulled me to my feet. "Are you hurt? What happened?"

We climbed into the cab.

"I couldn't see," I cried. "I couldn't see anything."

I heard you put the van in gear. You tried to go forward but it would not move. I felt the gears grind to reverse.

"No!" I shouted. "It's straight down! It's straight down!"

You got out to look.

"We're wedged against the boulder," you said.

"What do we do now?"

"We'll stay in the van until the storm blows over. Then we will have to walk to the cabin."

"Six miles?"

"Six miles."

"Won't we freeze tonight?"

"No. We have plenty of clothes. We'll run the heater for fifteen minutes every hour."

We huddled on the floor in the back, cuddled beneath layers of blankets and clothing. It was the closest I had felt to you in years.

"This reminds me of Grandpa Alistair," you said. "Did you know he slept with men?"

"What do you mean?" I asked.

"When he started the ranch and summered in a sheepwagon. He had a camptender. There's only one little bed in a sheepwagon. On cold or rainy nights they'd have to sleep together. He told me about it once when I was a kid. I think he was trying to shock me."

"What did you say, Donald?"

"I asked him how he could do it. Sleep that close to another man. He said: 'Laddie, you nevah knows where ya will make ya bed, or who ya will sleep with ifin it means ya saw-vival.' I guess he meant a person will do what he has to do to stay alive."

"Donald," I asked, "are we going to die?"

You chuckled, "No, of course not.

"Nope," you said proudly, "I've done about all I ever wanted to do. A farm. Good living. A cabin at the lake."

I wanted to say: What about our children? You hardly know them; and your father, Duncan, whom you seldom speak to? Or Clara? Or poor old Alistair alone in the nursing home?

You surprised me by breaking my imaginary conversation with a sudden laugh.

"What's so funny?" I asked.

"I was just thinking," you said. "I have one good reason not to die yet."

What? My hands became little fists of hope. Open your heart, Donald, I begged.

"I haven't published my book of poetry," you said. "I still hope to be on the 'Tonight Show.'"

Cold or not, I moved slightly away from you. You did not seem to notice. Silence blanketed us, and the buffeting of the wind against the side of the van seemed like the turning of blank pages in an unwritten book.

The silence was cold, but silence had always been cold with you even on the hottest summer day. I needed the warmth of words.

I thought of Grandpa Alistair lying like us, fragile and lonesome on a nursing home bed. His little shell rocked by strange winds. I wrote him weekly. I sent him a Bible. But like the others, I had not visited. I did pray for him often and wondered if he would die with murder in his heart.

"Donald?"

"Yeah?"

I was afraid to ask, but I had to. "Grandpa Alistair, do you think he killed that man?"

"Of course he did."

"I mean, on purpose."

I felt you shrug. "Might have, but the jury found him innocent."

Who was in the house when it happened? I tried to remember. His wife, Isabel. And Warren. Little Warren.

"Donald? What was the man's name?

"The Big Swede," you grunted.

"No," I said. "That's what everyone called him. But what was his name?"

I could feel you thinking, rolling Swedish surnames over in your head. "Hannson. Two *n*'s. Karl Hannson. Why?"

"No matter," I said. "Just wondering."

No matter? I asked myself. Of course it mattered. It mattered to Karl Hannson's wife. To his children. To the man who carved his tombstone. To Karl Hannson.

I slept fitfully. It was cold in the van. During the evening you rose about every half hour to run the engine and turn the heater on. But about nine o'clock you went to sleep and sawed logs straight through the night. I kept my head under my coat and tried to relax and think pleasant thoughts. In spite of your snoring, Donald, I managed to sleep a little, and at one point, I had a strange dream. I was Grandpa Alistair in the rest home and my pastor—the one you refuse to like—was sitting beside me reading from the Bible. He read Matthew 25:33: *"And He will set the sheep on His right hand, but the goats on the left."* And I rolled my eyes into my head and muttered: "Separation." That word was still on my lips when you jostled me awake at dawn.

"What are you doing, Donald?"

"Looking for clothes."

There was a metallic chill in the van. I rose from my coverings and pulled a curtain open on a side window. The stark brightness stabbed my eyes and made me draw back. The world was under eighteen inches of fresh snow and a brilliant yellow sun shone through a pass in the mountains. Creation seemed newly born in a crystalline purity.

"Where's my snowmobile suit?" you said. "I can't find it."

"It's a mile up the mountain, Donald. You threw it under the tires."

"Great. And my wool sweater?"

"It's probably up there, too. Along with your wool pants."

"What am I going to wear? I have six miles to hike and it must be ten below zero out there."

"Start the engine," I told you. "I will look for clothes."

The van cranked over slowly and I feared it was frozen, but it sputtered to life. I rummaged through the mess we had slept in. Fishing waders, raincoats, swimsuits, summer shirts, Bermuda shorts.

"What are you finding?" you asked.

"Swimsuits."

"Great."

"Donald," I said, "even if you make it to the cabin, what do we do then?"

"I'll call the ranger station. I will have them drive me back with the chains."

"Then what?"

"We'll have to go out the long way," you said. The long way was north, through a chain of low altitude passes and meadows. I had begged for that route yesterday. "That's two hundred miles out of our way," you had growled.

My fingers touched something that felt old and dead, like the hide of an animal. I pulled up something hairy and dirty yellow.

"We have these, Donald," I said.

"Chaps. Grandpa Alistair's old angora chaps." You seemed disgusted.

"What are these doing here?"

You shrugged. "I brought up some of Grandpa's old stuff, you know, in case anyone wanted me to do a poetry reading. I thought I would do it in period clothing."

The Tiberus Pass Historical Society, I remembered painfully. You were sure you would be selected to entertain at their annual summer banquet. Instead, they brought in an actor from Missoula who read Flathead Indian legends. My fingers moved to something soft and oily, like cool intestines. I dragged out an old shirt.

"Alistair's," you said. "It's a chamois shirt from France or somewhere. I was going to wear it with the chaps."

"Well, it's all I'm finding," I said. "Everything else must have been thrown under the tires."

You stared out at the bright morning. "Heavens, can't you find anything else? Nothing woolen?"

"Nothing."

You sighed deeply.

Wait, I thought, *there was one more thing.* I crawled to the back of the van and pulled a large plastic bag off a hanger. It was an old fur coat of Grandpa's, supposedly made in the twenties from the hides of the last wolves killed in Powder River County. He had wanted me to have it to wear, but it was musty and moth-eaten, and I accepted it only to please him.

"We have this," I said.

"Oh great," you muttered. "I hope all the bears have hibernated. Worse yet, I'll probably be adopted by some animal rights activist."

"There's nothing else," I said. "Except what you are wearing."

"Give me the chamois shirt," you said. "I will wear it under my jacket. And find me your sunglasses. It's terribly bright out there."

You pulled the shirt on as I searched for the glasses. Your own light ski jacket still was not going to be enough. You stared down at the deep carpet of snow-capped forest. "OK. Give me the chaps and fur coat."

You cussed and moaned as we buckled the angoras around your legs. They were heavy but warm. Then you bent over, and I pulled the wolf coat over your shoulders and you stabbed outwardly, pushing your arms through the sleeves.

"I feel like a goat that's been eaten by a wolf," you said.

You pushed the van door open and lumbered out, more like a bear leaving its den. You turned, looking back through wolf hair and sunglasses. "Run the van for ten minutes, then shut it off for twenty," you said. "Watch out if you feel sleepy, it might be monoxide poisoning."

I nodded. The morning air was icy cold and invasive.

"I will be back as soon as I can."

You moved around the front of the van, and I watched your progress through the windshield. Miles below you the Tiberus Valley lay stark and pristine. You began the long descent, your shoulders rounded by the burden of the coat, your legs thickened by angora hair.

And there you go, I thought, *my goat in wolf's clothing.* The creator of your own separation.

That was me. All of that really happened. Why had the Lord shown it to me again? Was He trying to validate the other revelations for me? I didn't know. I still don't know.

I put my hand on Donald's shoulder. "Sweetheart," I said, "they are serving the meal."

"I shouldn't eat," he said. "I should go to the men's room and work on the speech."

"Oh, Donald, I'm sure your speech will be fine."

He turned to me and assessed me through his rational gray eyes. "You don't understand," he said. "The speech has to be perfect. I have family here. Everyone knew Grandpa in their own way. They all have different expectations."

"Oh, I don't think it's that bad," I said.

"It is," he said, returning to his notes. He paused but did not look up. "Speeches like this are often a type of eulogy. Dead people are expected to be canonized. It's hard to make a saint out of old Alistair." He gave me his calculating, appraising look. "You," he said. "You got letters from the rest home before he died, letters the nurses wrote for him, did he say anything that I might be able to use in my speech?"

What did Grandpa say? I wanted to scream. I had all but begged Donald to read those letters. But he had refused, afraid that reading them would obligate him to write back. "He said a lot," I said.

"Well, like what?"

"Like he was tired and lonely and wished his family would visit."

"I can't use that," Donald said. "What else?"

"He thanked me for the Bible I sent and said his eyes were too dim to read but that an aide sometimes read it to him."

"Really? A Bible?"

"He mentioned Isabel a lot. He missed his wife. And he mentioned your mother, Martha, and your aunt Sarah."

"Oh? What did he say about them?'

"He just said that they were good women. Godly women."

Donald became very quiet but he did not quit thinking. No, his thinking intensified. And amplified. And I began hearing his voice. I decided to quit resisting the experience. Maybe I was going crazy, maybe it was all from Satan, but it was real, and in the end, the Lord would see me through it.

I decided I just had to trust God.

Besides, I was curious about what Donald would say.

9
Sermons

G odly women.

I met mine on Memorial Day, 1962, on the gravel road where her parents were killed. I was a hustling young real estate agent working out of Great Falls. As I rounded a curve on a barren stretch of country road I saw a lone figure, a pretty, young woman, kneeling at the road's side. She was tying flowers to an old cedar post. I nearly pushed the brake through the firewall on my '58 Chevy coming to a stop. "Do you know where the Larkin place is?" I asked.

"Why do you want to know?" she said.

"I'm a real estate agent. I hear it might be for sale."

"It's not," she said.

"How do you know?" I asked her.

"I own it," she said.

I had to let it sink in. She looked more like a high school cheerleader than a farm owner. "What are you doing?" I asked.

"Don't you know it's Memorial Day?" she said. "I'm marking the spot where my parents were killed three years ago."

"Oh," I said. Had I been embarrassed, I would have excused myself and driven away. But good salesmen don't embarrass easily.

"Do you always work on holidays?" she asked.

"I guess I forgot it was one, but yes, I usually work on holidays." She rose and brushed the dust from the knees of her denim pants. She wore a light flannel shirt and boots; her sandy blonde hair was pulled back in a ponytail.

"Where's your outfit?" I asked. There wasn't a car or truck in sight.

"I walked. My place is only a mile over that hill." Her arm stretched to a point. The sun glowed softly on her tanned cheeks. I offered her a ride and she accepted.

Her home—small, white, green shutters—was secluded behind a windbreak of elm and Russian olive trees. The farmyard was clean and well-traveled. Through the sliding doors of a Quonset hut I could see the large wheels of a tractor. Next to it sat three three-hundred-gallon fuel tanks mounted on a platform of railroad ties. One regular, two diesel. A waist-high white picket fence enclosed the grass, flowers, and doghouse of a woman's yard. A shaggy brown dog erupted from the doghouse barking furiously. My passenger ordered the dog to behave. It didn't. I got out of the car tentatively.

"Mercy doesn't like you," she joked.

"Mercy doesn't know me," I countered. But actually, that dog never did come to like me.

She told me thanks for the ride.

"You live here alone?" I asked.

"What if I do?" she said.

I shrugged. "Just wondering."

"I have a hired man."

I didn't say anything.

"He sleeps in the shop," she explained.

"How about if I take you out sometime?" I asked.

"I don't even know your name," she said.

"I'm Donald McColley."

"Where are you from?"

Mercy was sniffing me suspiciously. "Raised in Yellow Rock," I said. "Living in Great Falls now."

"Who told you my farm was for sale?"

"An implement dealer."

"I'll prove him wrong."

"Yes, I suppose you will," I said. "Now, what about our date?"

"I haven't even told you my name."

"You're Reba Larkin."

"Where are you going to take me?"

"Where do you want to go?"

"To church on Sunday."

Church? I absorbed it like a punch. "Sunday it is," I said. The dog started to growl softly. "Why did you name this dog Mercy?" I asked.

"Do you know a church hymn that goes: 'Surely goodness and mercy shall follow me all the days of my life'?"

"I've heard it," I said. I hadn't. But I would. A hundred times.

"After my folks were killed I got three pups. I named them Shirley, Goodness, and Mercy. Mercy is all I have left."

"Mercy's enough," I said. "See you Sunday." I drove away smiling at my good fortune. She was cute, plucky, and owned land.

"Are you a Christian?" she asked on our first date.

"Of course," I said.

"What faith?"

"I haven't really settled on any brand."

"What church were you raised in?"

"It didn't really have a name," I said.

"I know the type," she said, thinking I meant the tiny white community churches that dot the rural landscape of Montana, rising from a sea of prairie grass like cross-topped lighthouses. Her church was one of those. The congregation was mostly female. The few men that attended stood in the back and talked weather, grain prices, and tractors. Four different pastors rotated Sundays. In the summer everyone stayed after the service and had a potluck dinner out back. Mountains of food piled on old picnic tables.

Church was the only place she would let me take her, and she liked to sit up front, close to the preacher, which was a holy fright for me. During the song service we would each hold one side of the hymnal and her head drifted back, her eyes closed, and music trilled from her lips. Reba could sing. Still can. I kept my head down and mouthed the words. I pretended to look at the songbook but I was watching her. Adorned with devotion, she was a beautiful sight. I used to think: *Jesus, you have her now, but one day that look will belong to me.*

Months went by. I made a confession of faith and was baptized in Elkhorn Creek. Coming up out of the water, the first thing I saw was her face shining at me like a harvest moon. I proposed that night.

I set out to put the McColley plan to action, as Grandpa had defined it for me: marry an honest woman, then work hard for money because money is freedom. We worked hard. But Reba couldn't take it. She unraveled. The summer the Big Swede was killed I came home from Great Falls to find a tractor idling in the front yard. In the house the television was on, water was running in the sink, both babies were crying, and Reba was curled up like a cat in her mother's old wicker rocking chair. The noon dishes hadn't been done, let alone supper being made.

When I asked her what was going on, she just looked through me like she was reading a calendar on the wall.

"What's your problem?" I asked her.

She began jibbering about voices. Things about God and church and the devil. She was like that all night. Come morning I finally had to call a doctor.

The doctor recommended a week of bed rest in the hospital.

"A week!" I said. "Who's going to take care of the kids and cook for the men?"

"Do you have neighbors who could help?" he asked.

I was ashamed to admit I didn't. I hadn't been getting along with my neighbors very well.

"Then I guess you will have to do it," he said.

"But I'm too busy."

"Then hire someone."

"That costs money," I said.

"I suppose it does," he said. He was an old paternal-looking fellow, and he gave me an old paternal look. "Mr. McColley, your wife is up at 4 A.M. cooking, then she takes the children and sits a tractor till noon. When she comes home, she cooks again. Then she's out in the field all afternoon before cooking supper. Then she does dishes, bathes the children, and cleans house."

"So?" I asked.

"So she's exhausted. She needs some rest."

"Work never killed nobody," I said.

"Work kills everybody," he answered. "It's only a matter of how long it takes. But in your wife's case, I think there is an answer."

"What's that? Some expensive medicine?" I asked.

"No. Church."

You could have blowed me over with a grasshopper's sneeze.

"It's all she talked about this morning," he said. "When was the last time you let her go to church?"

"She gets there every couple of months," I said.

"Well, it's your wallet," he said. "It seems to me church would be a lot cheaper than hospitals and medicine. She needs strength. Evidently, she finds it in church."

So I let Reba go back to church. It seemed like the practical thing to do. The little country church closed down, so I let her drive to Great Falls on Sundays. Every couple of months I would go with her to see what she was getting into as she tried different churches. We went to a charismatic church one Sunday and Reba went forward for prayer, then dropped like a rock when the preacher touched her. I ran down to the altar and pulled her to her feet.

"She's OK," the preacher tried to tell me.

"The heck she is," I said. "A McColley lays down for nobody." I wasn't going to tolerate any strangeness.

Finally I got her to settle on a safe little church. Things went fine for a long time. I went to church on Christmas and Easter, and Reba and the kids went every Sunday, but they were always home to work in the afternoon. The church got the baby-faced new pastor fresh out of Bible school. He started on the "born-again" business and got people all stirred up. He made Reba their song leader and the kids started going to a youth group. I didn't mind them having a little religion if it helped them fly straight, I just didn't want it to interfere with life. But they got as radical as their mother.

I began to think I was losing the war. Grandpa, my father, and my uncle Roland never let things get this far.

Like a slow leak from a radiator, my engine began to overheat. I got curious about the books Reba was reading and the tapes she was listening to. Some Sunday mornings after everyone left for church I went back in the house and watched Kenneth Copeland on TV. I liked him. He reminded me of Grandpa Alistair in a

religious sort of way. But I turned the set off if he began
rattling in tongues.

Strange thoughts began entering my head. I wondered what death was like. Where would I go? I'd
always figured I was as good as the next guy, but a new
word had entered my mind. Sin. I'd heard altar calls
before but thought they were for others. I'd been
baptized in Elkhorn Creek. What more was there?

I knew there had to be more. I began remembering
the Bible lessons my grandma, Isabel, and my mother,
Martha, used to tell me. Maybe they'd been right after
all. The question of sin haunted me. I felt like a fox
with his tail on fire.

One Sunday I shocked my family and went to church.
Reba was up front leading the song service. Her usual
singing partner was gone so she was alone. Junior and
Donna were volunteering in the nursery. I didn't mind
sitting by myself. It seemed to take some pressure off.
Then before the singing started the preacher went to
the microphone and said: "Are there any sinners out
there?" He said it real loud so everyone could hear.

But only one person had to hear him. I knew he
meant me.

"Are there any sinners out there?"

I was a sinner.

Something seemed to lift me right out of that pew.
The entire congregation gasped as I moved forward. I
thought Reba was going to drop like a rock again. The
preacher's mouth was hanging on his chest. For once
in his life he seemed at a loss for words.

I stood at the altar. I didn't know what to do. Was I supposed to kneel? The preacher took me by the arm and led me up on stage. Then he handed me the microphone. *Oh, great,* I thought, *I have to make a public confession of my sin.* What would I admit? All the cheating I had done on land deals and taxes? The anger I felt toward my father? My bitterness toward my sister?

Then the pianist began playing.

Mood music, I figured.

The overhead projector came on. The words to a song I did not know appeared like handwriting on the wall. *Humble yourself in the sight of the Lord,* it read.

Well, I wanted to, if they would have just given me the chance. Then Reba began singing and nodding at me as she sang.

What did she want me to do? Scream my confession over the words of the song? I stood there as dumb as a new lamb in a snowstorm.

The preacher came up to me. "Is your mike working OK?" he asked.

I didn't know.

He fumbled with it. "It's fine," he said. "Go ahead and sing."

Sing?

Reba was already on a new song and was raising her hand. Was she waving at someone? Did she want to ask a question? I wanted to ask some questions. Did I have to raise my hand?

She nonchalantly came to me. "Sing, sweetheart," she said. "That's why you came up here."

Sing? I came to repent.

The second song ended. I was still standing like a post. "Donald," Reba whispered. "If you're scared, just mouth the words."

Scared? I was humiliated. They wanted me to sing. For the first time in my life I was truly embarrassed. I held the microphone as far from me as I could and lip-synched the words. Seven songs. It was the longest morning of my life. I wanted to run off that stage.

When I finally got to sit down, I couldn't concentrate. I never heard the preacher's message. As we left the church, people were patting me on the back and telling me how brave I was.

"Dad was singing up front!" The kids couldn't believe it.

"What made you do that, Dad?" Donna asked.

I shrugged.

Later, when we were alone, Reba asked me: "Donald, when the pastor asked if there were any singers out there, what prompted you to come up?"

Are there any singers out there?

I thought he said: *Are there any sinners out there?* But I didn't tell Reba. I just said: "You looked lonely up there all by yourself."

She kissed me on the cheek. "That was sweet," she said. After that she seemed to have hope for me. She invited me to read the Bible with her. I declined. She would ask if we could say grace at the table. That was OK. She hinted about me praying with her. I said I was too busy. But the guilt never left; it just changed into anger and bitterness. I was jealous of Jesus. But it wasn't my fault. It was the preacher's.

I never forgave him for my embarrassment. *Are there any singers out there?* How foolish! How unprofessional! They should teach better diction in those Bible schools.

I know Reba thinks I will come forward again sometime. Maybe. She thinks deep down inside me there is something rare and valuable waiting to be discovered. Could be. But chances are she would have more luck looking for Grandpa's buried gold.

Are there any sinners out there? Oh, Donald, I never realized how close to salvation you had come. I reached over and squeezed his arm. "I love you," I said.

He looked at me curiously. "What was that for?" he said.

"Nothing," I smiled. "I just want you to do well on your speech."

"I wish they'd never picked me," he said. "After all, most of the real interesting things about Alistair were controversial, like the killing of the Big Swede, his buried money, him being an atheist who dies with a Bible on his chest."

He died with a Bible on his chest? How did Donald know that? The insights I had been given could naturally make me suspicious. Had Donald been reading the letters after all? Had he even visited Grandpa in Yellow Rock? I shook the thoughts off. The Lord has warned me not to judge, not to be presumptuous. The more I knew, the less I wanted to know.

"What are you shaking your head for?" he asked.

"Oh, I was just thinking that it was a shame that the kids couldn't be here. I know you will give a great speech."

"Yeah, I wish the kids were here."

"Maybe the speech can be taped," I said.

"Tape it. Now there's an idea. Why didn't I think of that?"

"I will go ask a museum official," I said. "Be right back."

They were serving the meal and Donald was to speak immediately afterward. I had to hurry. There were thirty or forty guests in the building. A few stopped me to talk and I know I was courteous, but I don't remember a word I said. I was in a different world. I excused myself from each by saying I was on an errand. I needed a recorder. The only museum person I could locate was standing at the bar next to Dick and Pete. I explained to him what I wanted. As we talked I overheard the discussion behind me. Dick was getting drunk.

"Hey, Pete," I heard him say, "what's the deal with you and Clara? You two married or what?"

"Could be," Pete said.

"Ha. With your luck the old man ain't dead. Old Duncan's just hidin' out in the hills—probably huntin' Grandpa's gold—any day he'll come back and find the two of you together."

"I'm not worried about Duncan," Pete said.

Dick paused. I could hear him swirl the ice in his drink. "Some people think you know where the body is."

"People are always thinkin' things they don't know," Pete said.

"There's even a few who think you killed him."

There was an eerie silence, like the instant before thunder claps. I could feel the chill in Pete's stare.

Dick laughed, and I heard him slap Pete's shoulder. "Just joshin' ya, buddy," he said.

"I can't say murder is all that funny," Pete said. He turned and walked away. I watched him walk to where Clara was sitting.

"Can you beat that?" Dick said to himself. "Pete Andraxie all mothered-up and on the wagon."

The museum man said it could be arranged. It would take only a few minutes to set up a recorder. I thanked him.

"Strange things," I heard Dick say. "Strange things sure do happen in this world."

I rejoined Donald. I told him he would be recorded and he was pleased.

"Strange things," I heard Dick say. "Strange things sure do happen in the world . . ."

10
The Tumbleweed

I have a story to tell and no one to tell it to. Pete's mothered-up with Clara. Marci's back to jawin' with Reba. Church-talkin' again, no doubt. Donald's workin' on the Speech of Destiny.

My story causes me pain with every breath. You see, I have six broken ribs wrapped tighter than snakeskin.

It all started after the Rooster died. My father had no will, so the ranch was sold on the courthouse steps. I had hopes of buyin' it. One hope. Alistair. I went to see him. He was all withered up, nothin' left but husk.

"Grandpa," I said, "I need to talk to you about money."

"Done buried it," he cackled.

"I need money to buy Dad's ranch," I said.

"Buried it," he laughed. His teeth were gone and his skin was the color of old newspaper, but a fierce energy still brewed in the old man.

"Where did you bury it?" I asked.

"Buried it fifteen years ago. No one ever find it."

I tried to stir his memory. "Fifteen years ago," I said. "You took the money from the sale of your ranch and disappeared for three days. Do you remember, Grandpa?"

"How's the sheep market?" he asked.

"Think, Grandpa. Try to remember. You were gone three days. The sheriff found you sitting in your truck on a county road miles from your ranch. You were delirious and dehydrated. Your ankle was broken. Where had you been, Grandpa?"

"The Old Country," he said. "I want to see the Old Country." Scotland. He was talkin' about Scotland. I was talkin' about gold.

"Grandpa, do you know that the Rooster is dead? Your son, Roland, he's dead."

"Buried it," he cackled. "No one find it."

"They are gonna sell his ranch," I said.

"Buried it, buried it in a baking powder tin."

"Where? Where did you bury it?"

"Reba writes me letters."

"I know, I know. Reba writes everyone letters." Then I had a strange idea. "Grandpa," I said, "Did you tell Reba where the money is buried?"

"Reba knows."

"Reba knows where the money is?" I was panicked. If Reba knew, then Donald knew. If Donald knew, the money was long gone.

"Reba knows Jesus," he said.

"Jesus? What about the money? Did you tell Reba where the money was?"

"Buried it," he laughed. "Mother's Love."

Mother's love. What did that mean? The old man had to be nuts.

"Gold. All gold. Don't believe in paper money," he said in wisps of breath. He seemed to be gettin' a little excited.

"Shh," I said. "Lie still and be quiet." I was afraid the old guy would have a heart attack on me. That would have made two for the year. I looked around the room nervously. There was very little there. An old photo of his dog, Queenie. A stack of letters from Reba. A Bible.

The letters! I took one, opened it, and read it, hopin' to find a mention of the money. It wasn't the right thing to do, but the ranch was at stake.

I read several letters, but there was no mention of the money. All Reba talked about was God. That was more than I could take. I knew Alistair wasn't gonna help me. "I have to go, Grandpa," I said.

"Buried it," he laughed. "Gold. Baking powder. No one ever find it."

Eight months later the ranch was sold. Marci and I hit the road again. It tore my guts out to leave the ranch I had grown up on. I'd left before but always counted on comin' back. *It's just a chunk of earth*, I told myself.

I had nothin', thanks to my grandfather who had buried his gold; thanks to my father who had left no will.

That night I got drunk in the Buffalo Bar in Yellow Rock. Somebody told me about a job up near Plentywood. They said it was a cowboy kind of outfit, an oldtimer with a herd of snotty Longhorn cattle. I dug deep for quarters and called the guy.

"You ain't a rodeo bum are ya?" the man asked.

"I do my cowboyin' in the hills," I told him.

"You can handle rank stock?"

"I can," I said. The man's voice sounded like a death rattle. I was hopin' he wouldn't die before I got employed.

"Wahll, come on up," he said.

We were there the next day. I got worried as we drove in because of two big Allis-Chalmers tractors sittin' in the yard. Marci would not even look at them. She knows I won't farm. I'd swamp bars before I'd be a tractor jockey.

Robinson wasn't as old as he sounded. "I won't do any farmin'," I told him.

"Ya won't have to," he said. "The farmin' is all in CRP now. Just clippin' coupons from the government," he smiled.

The house wasn't much, but they never are. Wages were just enough to keep a couple poor.

Robinson wore a battered felt hat, cowboy boots, and an oversized set of bib overalls. Chewin' tobacco dripped off his chin like Exxon had wrecked a tanker in his mouth.

He led us down to the corral to take a look at his horses. An old broken-down sorrel had to be his. The rest were young and wolfy-lookin', with slender necks and heads as long as fenceposts. They pinned their ears and watched me through the whites of their eyes.

The corrals were crumblin', held together with bailin' twine and promises. I knew my first work would be to rebuild the pens, then take the howl out of his horses.

"My cattle are Longhorns crossed with horned Herefords," he said. "They tend to have poor dispositions."

Three days later Robinson left to spend the winter—and his CRP money—in Arizona. Marci and I settled in for the winter.

I never got the word on Grandpa's death or Uncle Duncan's disappearance until days after the fact. No one knew where we were. One morning I heard a radio report about a missing rancher named McColley. I called Clara right away, and she told me about her dad being lost. I knew he was dead. This country don't forgive mistakes.

Then she told me Grandpa Alistair had died. The funeral was over but no one had been there.

"He probably carried his own casket to his grave," I joked.

I didn't feel any real sorrow. I just felt cut off. Set adrift. My father, Grandpa Alistair, Uncle Duncan . . . all dead. It seemed like there was some sort of curse on the McColley men. I wondered if I'd be next.

Marci said there was a curse. A curse of unbelief. "Our life is meant to be fruit and flowers, and it's nothing but weeds," she said. Whatever that meant.

Weeds I understood. Especially thistles.

CRP stands for Conservation Reserve Program. It should stand for Communistic Ranch Practices. It's a government program to seed marginal farmland back to grass. But, the first couple of years the only thing that grows is Russian thistles. Tumbleweeds. They grow bigger than beachballs, then break off in the wind and bounce away, hundreds at a time. A real weed stampede. They cover fences, catch snow, and lay the fence down.

Robinson came back in March, tanned and ornery, and the first thing he saw was tumbleweeds that covered all the fencelines. "Stack 'em and burn 'em," he ordered.

Stack 'em and burn 'em. That meant work with a pitchfork. Might as well be the devil in hell as to stand pitchin' weeds in a fire. It was the same as bein' a farmer.

I was real quiet at lunch but a lot can be said in silence. Marci wore her worried look and tiptoed around my nervousness. I wolfed the meal down and headed back out. She stopped me at the door, gave me a hug and smiled weakly. It was her way of sayin': *If you want to go, I'm ready to pack.* That only made it worse. I had to show her I didn't quit that easily.

Marci's done a lot of changin' the past couple of years. Her sass and spunk has dimmed considerable. Maybe it's this religion stuff. Or maybe she is just tired. She ain't as quick to fight, that's for sure.

I went to work stackin' and burnin' but my mind drifted. I thought about the best saddle broncs I'd ever rode and the scores I'd marked: seventy-six on Mooncat at Stanford; eighty on Barstool at Winnett. I rode 'em again in my mind with Marci watchin' from the fence, the reins to her barrel horse danglin' from her hand. It made me feel alive.

By day's end I was saddle sore in my mind rememberin' Wee Willie Watson, a city boy who wanted to ride bareback horses in the worst way. That's how he done it, too. In the worst way. Wee got to the rodeo grounds early, parked his pickup near the chutes, then sat there listenin' to Chris LeDoux rodeo songs that shook his little Toyota like a beer can. The other cowboys were loosenin' their bodies. Wee Willie worked on his mind.

I always set the riggin' for him. When the chute boss screamed his name, Willie would fly outa the truck, climb down on his horse and yell, "Let's make music!"

He'd last about two jumps then come crashin' down on his head, the music spillin' out all over the ground.

That's the way dreams leave us. Not with a whisper in the night but with a thunderous crash. My ache for land was the sound of a dream dyin'.

I forked weeds for five days straight, stinkin' of smoke, gasoline, and sweat. I did it for Marci.

When the fences were clear, Robinson showed up again.

"We gotta prolapsed cow in the ragweeed pasture," he said. The "we" meant the cow was his, but the problem was mine. He told me to saddle the zebra-striped dun.

We were experiencin' a winter thaw and the ground was ice in some places, snow in others, and mud in between. The dun wasn't sharp-shod, so I headed out barefoot on a bronc. It was noon when I left.

A prolapse is when a cow pushes her uterus out. It hangs under her tail like a big red ball. If she's already calved, it's no big deal. You just rope her, throw her, push the ball back in and stitch her up. If she hasn't calved, you take her to a vet and he puts a thingamajig in her that holds the uterus in and still lets her calve. This cow hadn't calved yet. I had to find her, trail her some six miles home, then load her and haul her to town. No big deal.

The dun was responsive and spirited, a good traveler. I eased him from a fast walk into a trot. It felt good bein' horseback. The weather was mild, I was away from the tumbleweeds and my only concern was time. The days were short.

I was lucky in findin' the cow. She was a bunch-quitter that likes the big lonesome country. She spied me from a distance, stuck her tail in the air, and took to runnin'. I could see her red ball bouncin' up and down. Me and the dun had to cut a fast, wide swath to get around her.

The ol' cow wanted nothin' to do with goin' home and took a run or two at me. I shook my lariat down and slapped her longside the head a couple times. That educated her and she lined-out down a fenceline at a brisk trot. I knew she was apt to get tired, hot, and on the fight, but I had to let her travel her own pace. I relaxed and enjoyed the day.

I was thinkin' about Uncle Duncan and what would come of his place—I figured Donald would find a way to get it away from Clara—when we came to a problem: a gate, then a steep trail uphill. The trail was on the shady side of the hill and was glossy with ice. Cows hate ice. This one hated gates too, and made her own hole in the fence. When I dismounted, she watched me from fifty feet through red, calculatin' eyes. Slobber hung from her mouth like spider webs, and her sides heaved in quick bursts, her breath blowin' out like steam. She jerked her head around, looked up the hill, then back at me. I've got enough cow in me that I can read trouble. I led my horse through the gate and remounted.

"Come on, ol' girl," I coaxed the cow, sweet-talkin' in my nicest voice while I tickled the dun forward with my spurs. The cow eyed the fence, then eyed me and I read her little bovine mind and built me a loop. "You aim for that fence and I'm gonna rope your sorry hide," I told her. She shook her head angrily. She was rope-wise. Like a lady, she turned and tried the hill, and I spurred the dun to encourage her. But not being sharp-shod, the dun was slippin'. The cow fell to her knees three times. The third time she rose with a whole new attitude. I tried to rush her, but the dun couldn't collect his feet so I lashed at her with my rope. The cow turned and charged. It was a heart-weakener for both me and the dun to see a set of horns headed downhill with a thousand pounds of cow behind them. Not havin' the footin' to pivot, the horse reared.

The cow hit the dun and I felt his back hooves give. In an instant we were in the soup, a tangle of horse, cow, rider, and rope crashin' down the hill. I felt the hard ground rise up and smack me and the thrashin' of the dun's legs around my head as he fought to get to his feet.

I tried to roll free of rope and animals, but the fence stopped us. The horse righted himself and plunged through the fence, the wires singin' as they snapped.

I rolled to a crouch. The cow was uphill from me but slidin' slowly my way like a big leather sled. I coiled my legs to jump but she sprung to her feet and hit me just as I lifted off the ground. The momentum carried both of us backward, me on my back, the cow on her knees until I was stopped by the solid strength of a railroad tie. I struggled to my feet, dazed. She hit me again, her narrow head crashin' into my ribs, her wide-angled horns juttin' to either side of me like railin's. She slammed me against the fencepost, knockin' the wind from my lungs.

This is gettin' rather serious, I told myself. Matters were becomin' intimate. Her heaviness weighed on me and I could feel her breath and smell her hair. And I could taste her madness. She kept pushin' me forward tryin' to overpower the fencepost that stood between her and escape, and I was sandwiched in the middle, her horns pinnin' my arms to my sides. My first rib cracked; a sudden weakness followed by a hot, flarin' pain. My mouth formed a scream, but no words came as my chest and lungs were filled with cow. She pushed desperately as if it were her life on the line and from the corner of my left eye I saw why. Her horn had imbedded into a crack in the heavily creosoted railroad tie. I looked to my right. The other horn's long curled tip had snaked through a loop in the wire. The cow was captured.

A whole side of my ribs caved in like dirt off a cutbank. I thought I heard the pops as the bones broke. *So this is how I die,* I thought. The wreck was only minutes long but already felt like hours. The cow thought so, too. I could feel her tirin'. The friction of her hooves against the frozen gumbo was softenin' and slickenin' the ground, givin' her less of a base to propel herself from. I felt a hot moisture around my groin. Had I wet myself or was it just slobber from the cow? I didn't know and I didn't care.

It was a cowboy way to die, I figured, but I wasn't too keen on the timin'.

I couldn't die before ownin' my own place.

I struggled, but was pinned by pain, horns, and the weight of the cow. I whispered curses at her. Stupid mindless brute. If she had pulled backward she might've gotten free but she kept pushin' forward, killin' me in the process.

My hands brushed against the cool metal of my chaps' buckle, and I unfastened it with thick fingers. The cow sensed the movement and renewed the attack. Her nose thrust into my thigh, pullin' the chaps down. She seemed heavier. I could smell her anger and see the red ball of her prolapse swingin' from one hip to the other. She butted me in the stomach. I heaved, sprayin' her neck and shoulders with vomit while feelin' the splinters of ribs rise, align, and point themselves toward my heart.

I forced my hand inside the left pocket of my jeans and grasped my pocket knife. The cow's weight shifted, pinnin' my hand in my pocket. My fingers felt thick and numb. Suddenly, in a fit of fury, she tried shakin' her head free and that gave me an inch of margin to pull the knife out. I clenched it, unopened, in my fist.

The cow relaxed. I heard her lungs drawin' air. Carefully, I moved my left hand across my crotch, prayin' not to provoke her. My thumbnail found the grooved notch on the knife's longest, sharpest blade. I pried the blade open, grippin' the handle with the last of my strength. Lookin' down at the white and red cowhide, I guessed at the locations of the jugular, braced myself, and stabbed. The cow bellered in a rage. The blade was in her but the weight and force of her strength was wrestlin' the knife from my hand. I pushed down, feelin' tissue give way beneath the keen steel edge. Somethin' thick and warm coated my hands. Blood.

She pummelled me with knees, hooves, and the noise of her bellerin', but I managed to hold tight and let her fury move against the blade until the knife finally dropped from my hand. A geyser of blood arched out from the cow, sprayin' me and the fencepost; coatin' and drippin' from strands of wire. The spray pulsed with the heartbeat and effort of the cow and dimmed as she did. Her death rattle escaped in my face, and she pulled me down in her collapse, the burden of her carcass settlin' on my legs and stomach like half a ton of wet blankets. The blood slowed to a thick, syrupy flow that lacquered my chaps and legs.

The cow died, her head uplifted by the hold on her horns, her lathered face in my lap.

Now, for the first time, I felt the terror of my situation. I saw the cold blue hills stretchin' to a darkenin' skyline. I felt the chill of night fallin' like a curtain and counted the distance home, the hours of waitin'. My legs felt thick and lifeless, as if paralyzed, but I was able to flex my thigh muscles. The cow had me pinned to the fence like a tumbleweed. I imagined Robinson findin' me and the cow.

"Stack 'em and burn 'em," he'd say.

My best hope was the horse. Would he go straight home or just drift north and stand stupidly in the far corner of the pasture? In any case, Marci would come lookin' for me sooner or later. She'd get nervous about dark and debate about callin' Robinson. She'd figure I'd want him left out of it, so she'd climb in the truck and come lookin'. The night would be moonlit. Marci would find me. She was a tough country girl. A good hand.

The cold began slippin' in from all sides—I wanted my hat but it was on up the hill a ways—but the blood freeze-dried on my legs had an insulatin' effect. I got feelin' a little sick, like my innards weren't quite right.

Well, dang, I thought, just maybe I won't ever have a place of my own. I didn't think much about death itself. I figure when you're dead, you're dead. That's what Grandpa Alistair always used to say. Plant 'em and forget 'em.

There were lots of things I was wantin' to forget. Like makin' the Rooster hop and forcin' Marci to have an abortion. Forgettin' has usually been easy for me. But most of all I didn't want to think about religious things.

Grandma had religion, but Grandpa kept it stifled. Same for my mother and my aunt. That's one thing about us McColleys: we either marry religious women or livin' with us makes 'em that way. Now Marci had the bug. Too many letters from Reba. Now she's drivin' fifty miles to church or listenin' to tapes all day. She got me to church once. I sat there stiff and cold, countin' hypocrites and wishin' I was out in the hills. The preacher preached outa some book called Ax. Somethin' about Paul arguin' with some stoics and cynics and the preacher said God was still warrin' 'gainst them attitudes. At the end, people went down to the front for prayer, but I didn't believe none of it, and if I had, I wouldn't've let anyone know. Book of Ax. Strange name for a Bible book. Wonder if they have one called Book of Shovel?

Like Grandpa said: religion is for old women and babies, and as for preachers, he called 'em too lazy to work and too scared to steal.

I had no way of trackin' time. The chill set in more, and I figured that hyperthermia stuff would get me. I hoped Marci hadn't snuck off to church. What night was it? Sunday? No. It was Wednesday. I told her she couldn't go to church on Wednesday nights anymore. Had she listened?

I was in a little bit of shock and an awful lot of pain. It hurt to breathe, but it hurt more thinkin' about not breathin'. I was darn cold, and my blood wasn't circulatin' well. I didn't know if I was bleedin' inside or not.

Funny thoughts began movin' through my head like my brain was a television set tuned to the Saturday mornin' cartoons. I could see things and hear them, but they didn't look quite real. They began takin' shape around me in the darkness.

"If you come to visit," I told 'em, "lend a hand and pull this cow off."

Heck, it's odd what your brain can do when your body is under stress.

I thought I saw a black man step outa the darkness. Outside of seein' the Rooster come back from the dead that's about the last thing I wanted to see. He seemed to stare at me a long time, his arms folded across his chest while I tried to get my eyes focused. He was tall and bald and muscled and didn't look like any one black man in particular. He looked like all of them rolled into one.

"Why did you do what you did?" he asked.

I twisted hard tryin' to get away but I was captive, like I was trussed-up, manacled, and held by guards.

"Why does it bother you to question your motives?" he asked.

"Heck, man," I said. "It was a joke. We'd been drinkin' three days. There weren't no motives."

He stood there, hands on his hips, the whites of his eyes shinin' like little headlights. "Why did you do it?"

"Man, like I said, we'd been drinkin' three days. My father had just fired me. Marci was threatenin' to leave me. I just needed to blow off some steam. I don't remember everythin' that happened."

"Would you like me to remind you?"

"You got off a Greyhound bus and came in the bar," I told him. "You thought it was a cafe. It was just a joke, that's all."

"Did I laugh?" the black giant asked.

I couldn't answer him at first. The blackness was inky dark above me, with his muscles outlined like a blue horizon. The white headlights of his eyes drew slowly closer.

"Did I laugh?"

"No! You didn't laugh. We didn't give you time. You were smaller then. One of the boys grabbed you."

"Did you stop him?"

"No."

"Did you help him?"

"I don't know."

"You don't want to know. What did you do next?"

"They tied you up—"

"You tied me up."

"I tied you up. They wrestled you down. I tied you with a curtain sash."

"And then what did you do?"

"They did it. They picked you up, carried you outside and threw you in the back of Pete's pickup. Pete said he didn't want anythin' to do with it. But he came along."

He moved closer. He seemed to be darkness itself. "It was cold out, wasn't it?" he said.

"Twenty below, but we couldn't feel nuthin'."

"Where did you take me?"

"To the Hide and Fur Depot. The place that buys pelts."

"Why?"

"Because it was a joke. They said you were a coon."

"Who went in?"

"I went in and talked to the manager. Pete said we should let you go, but the rest of us were all carried away with it by then."

He leaned closer and his eyes seemed to shine into the bottom of my soul. "What did you tell the manager?" he asked.

"I said, 'You buyin' furs?' And he said he was. 'How 'bout coon?' I asked. He said he was. 'Follow me,' I said. 'We got the biggest coon you ever did see.'"

"And?" The eyes were as big and bright as hubcaps now.

"He came out to the truck and looked down and saw you layin' in there all tied up, your eyes big and white like they are now. 'Get him outa there!' he screamed."

"And?"

"The manager and Pete, they set you free and you took outa there runnin' like a scalded cat. But it was just a joke. I didn't come to my senses for a couple days. I didn't even remember any of it."

The eyes pulled back, becomin' about the size of silver dollars. "What happened in Saigon?" he asked.

"Man, you can't know about that."

He nodded. "I know. Tell me."

"I was a Marine embassy guard when Saigon fell to the Commies. Me and my best friend were up on the roof, loadin' dinks into a chopper . . ."

"And?"

"This crazy dink, an Army officer I think, he came runnin' at us with a big knife. He knew there wasn't room for him, but he was gonna force his way on. I was loadin' a pregnant woman. He pushed her away. She stumbled and fell into the crowd, and all I could see was the pregnant dink lady disappearin' under a stampede of feet."

"And?"

"I reached down to help the lady, blockin' the guy's way onto the bird. He raised the knife to stab me. I looked up too late. I saw the blade comin' down, straight for my heart. Then Anthony shot him. Point-blank in the head with his M-16. Brains and blood scattered everywhere."

"And?"

"And Anthony was a Negro, OK? You know that. You know when I dream about tyin' you up I look down in the truck bed, the manager of the fur depot screamin' in my ear, and I see you and you become Anthony, and I wonder how I could have done that. He was my best friend."

"Anthony was your best friend, " he said. "But who am I?"

"I don't know," I screamed. "Who are you?"

He laughed, his teeth shinin' pearly-white as piano keys. "I am the darkness within you," he said. "I visit you at night."

He stepped back, and the darkness seemed to wane
with him. The whites of his eyes receded until they were
only the size of dimes. They were high above me, on a
hill, or lookin' down from heaven itself. I was cold but
feverish. Sweat ran down my brow and froze my cheeks.
Maybe I cried. I can't remember. But I found breath
to scream.

"Anthony!" I called. "Anthony!"

I screamed at those dime-sized lights that shone above
me.

"Anthony! Anthony!"

Marci came.

She nosed the four-wheel drive out over the edge of
the hill pointin' the headlights downward. In the beam
she saw me, a single figure covered by cowhide and
blood, pinned to a fencepost as large as a tree.

I was still screamin': "Anthony! Anthony!" when she
came with the horn saw to cut me free.

"Anthony! Anthony!"

"Dick, this isn't a dream," she said. "This is real."

"Reba, I could use a drink," Donald said. I did not
hear him.

I was swirling in a world where men watched other
men die, where the joy and sensitivities of the child are
ripped like little flowers from the soul and hung to
wither on the barbed-wire fences of our own dreams and
the expectations of others. I was still in the world of
Dick McColley. A violent, sad, masculine world survived
only through a perverse sense of humor.

"I'm sorry, Donald, what did you say?"

"I said I could use a drink. My nerves are shot. Maybe a glass of wine to drink with the meal."

"OK," I said. I never worried about Donald and drinking. He was very temperate. He didn't like to lose control.

I returned to the bar. Dick was there alone. I asked the bartender for a glass of wine.

"So, Reba," Dick said, "did you come over to have a drink with me?"

"No, Dick. I'm getting Donald a glass of wine for his nervous stomach."

"Afraid of makin' the speech, ain't he? Well, I suppose I would be, too. But I have a great story to tell. Want to hear a good story?"

I wanted to tell him I already heard it. But I didn't. "I don't really have time right now," I said.

"So you won't have a drink with me?"

"Dick, you know I don't drink."

"How about letters? You ever write letters?" he asked sarcastically.

I didn't answer him. He was drunk enough to be volatile.

"Reba of the letters. Is there a Book of Reba in the Bible? There should be."

Please, Bartender, bring the wine, I thought.

Dick's handsome face turned into a gruesome sneer. "You filled Marci's head with all that religion stuff, didn't you? Heck, I liked her better the way she was. How about Clara? You writin' her letters too? I heard you were writin' Grandpa Alistair. Did he tell ya where his gold was?"

"Bartender, my wine please," I said, but he was busy with an old man who didn't think his change was correct.

"Grandpa Alistair was right," Dick drawled. "Religion is for weaklings. Grandpa never would have no part of it. Now gold and land and cattle, them are things to believe in. Things to get your hands around." He moved closer to me. I backed up but hit a wall.

"Marci thinks we McColleys are cursed," he said. His breath smelled of liquor, and he seemed to swell in size like an angry badger. "What do you think?"

Before I could answer, Pete stepped between us. His presence moved Dick back a step. I sighed with relief. Pete ordered two grapefruit juices. Dick turned his attention to Pete, and I thanked God for his intercession.

"Hey, Andraxie," Dick said, "I got a good story to tell ya about this little wreck I was in."

"I noticed you're movin' a little stiff," Pete said.

"Yeah, I got sandwiched between a ringy old cow and a post . . ."

"Sounds like a baloney sandwich to me," Pete said.

The bartender brought me Donald's wine and I excused myself. Marci was gesturing to me as I moved through the tables, and I could not simply ignore her.

"It's happened again, hasn't it?" she said.

I didn't want to lie but I didn't want to talk about it either. I just looked at her vacantly.

"You had another vision or something. I could tell. Who was it about?"

Dick interrupted us. "Come on, Marci," he said. "We might as well sit down and get a free meal out of this. There sure isn't anyone interestin' to talk to here. Might as well eat."

"You could talk to Warren," she said. I knew she was only trying to get rid of Dick for a moment.

"Warren! Jeez, what would Warren have to talk about? Nothin' interestin' happens to Warren."

At the mention of his name I turned and stared past the tables of elderly guests and officials and found Warren, by himself, still seated at the table most distant from the wall where Alistair McColley's portrait hung. It was as if he heard his name because he looked up from his dinner and stared at us.

Or should I say he stared at me.

I have interesting stories to tell. I heard him say.

11
Bitter Roots

About three years ago, B.D.—before divorce—I developed an insatiable need to be around things western. I dreamed about Montana and awoke smelling branding fires and horse sweat. I bought *Western Horseman* magazines that sat on my office desk unopened and put Montana photographic posters on the walls.

Marge noticed the change immediately. "What latent longing is this?" she asked. "Some subconscious need to return to your roots?"

"What's the state flower of Montana?" I asked her, wielding the rapier-like tone to my voice that she so detested.

"I don't know. Cactus, I suppose."

"Bitterroot," I said.

Bitter root. She got it. Marge was always quick. "Sarcasm does not become you," she said, renewing a longstanding argument about my dry, cynical sense of humor. "What's the real reason for all of this sudden interest in your home state? Do you want to go home for a visit? Are we becoming compulsive-obsessive again?"

"Leave the psychological terms to me," I said.

"Well—"

"That's a deep subject."

"Cute," she said. "Now what exactly are you digging for?"

"Grandpa's gold."

"Sure, Warren. Escape in humor. Now, what is with this instant rural longing? Don't tell me you want to go visit your relatives."

Holy trauma! Did I? I hoped not. "Let's go to a rodeo," I said. That thought just jumped out, like a calf from a roping chute.

"A rodeo? You have to be joking." Marge hated rodeos. She considered them inhumane. She also had never been to one.

"Pendleton. There's the Pendleton Roundup."

She gave me her wise, all-knowing look, followed by a slight, upturned wrinkle of her lips that suggested she had her own angle. "OK," she said. "On one condition."

I rolled my eyes. Her conditions were always as heavy as anvils.

"There are some people in Pendleton I have been wanting to meet. I will go to your"—she added her own sarcastic inflection—"roe-day-oh with you if you come to the meeting with me."

"*Rode-ee-oh*," I corrected her. "What type of meeting?"

"You know what type."

I sighed heavily. An Ooohhh-eee, wooo-eeee type. Space cadets. New Age zombie masters.

"Deal?" she asked.

"What are they?" I demanded. "Witches? Warlocks? Mutant Amazon Warrior Women from Venus Who Did Not Shave Their Legs?"

"They are very respectable," she said. "As respectable as any *roe-day-oh*."

Horse trading with Marge was insufferable. She owned all the horses. She was Feminist-Vegetarian-Environmentalist-Animal Rightist-Reformed Socialist Turned Spiritualist. Her ante was a Ph.D. in political science, mine a master's in psychology, and she had paid for most of my education.

"OK," I said. "It's a deal."

She gave me her benign nod of approval, her blessing from the Moon Goddess. Her hair was pulled back tight and tied up off her shoulders. Mercy, she was beautiful when she wanted to be. She had a mind like a razor-edged coyote trap and the legs of a dancer. I had always been attracted to both ends of her wondrous body and everything in between.

We took a long, roundabout way to Pendleton, going east to Bend, then taking Highway 20 southeast to Burns through high desert ranch country and the Burns Indian Reservation. Then we pointed the little convertible north toward Pendleton.

"Again," quizzed Marge. "Why the *roe-day-oh*? She insisted on the Spanish pronunciation.

"I like to watch cowboys eat dust," I said.

"Ashes to ashes. Dust to dust. You miss your brother."

Low blow. Lower than my head but above the belt.

"He rode broncos, didn't he?"

"Broncs, not broncos. You are sounding like a dude," I told her. "What else, Dr. Margaret Talcott-McColley?"

"You have an inner conflict with your father that needs to be resolved."

"Who doesn't?" I said.

"The poet Robert Bly says no man is free until his father is dead."

"A reasonable argument for murder," I said.

"Your family has bad karma," Marge said. She turned her head to the scenery, using one hand to hold her raven-black hair out of her eyes as the Miata cut through the dry desert air.

"Get a Webster's," I told her. "Look up the word *dysfunctional*. It will say *see McColley family, Montana*."

"Bad karma," she said again. "You keep reincarnating to torture one another." She straightened her hand like a salute to shield her eyes from the sun. "It's like this beautiful desert," she said.

"It's reincarnating to torture my family?"

"No. More bad karma. White European males raped and exploited the Native Americans and the land itself. As the leaders of the nations, they are accountable for the karma. They will be judged for it."

"All problems are caused by white men?" I asked, baiting her. We had been over this ground countless times.

"Primarily. The symptoms of our social ills find their roots in the racism, imperialism, and sexism of the heterosexual white male. You know that."

"Judeo-Christian," I said. "You forgot Judeo-Christian heterosexual white male."

"The implication was obvious," she said.

"And now we have judgment coming?"

"One must reap what he sows."

"A biblical principle. You are using a biblical principle?" I asked, baiting her again.

"There are few elementary truths in the Bible: reaping, sowing, judgment. Though of course, fundamental, evangelical Christianity is the actual cause of most evil in the world."

"Judgment? You mean like AIDS? I think that one's for the gay—"

"Cut it, Warren. Don't be homophobic around me. You may be gay in your next incarnation if you are not careful. Besides, you know I was not making reference to hellfire-and-brimstone judgment. That is a ridiculous myth created by small and evil minds to control other small minds through the use of guilt."

I decided on a new attack. Closer to home.

"Imperialists," I said. "You mean people like your parents, the high and mighty Talcotts. They've made a fortune in resources. First in timber, then in real estate development in Portland. That money put you and me through school."

"Yes," she said. "Like the Talcotts. We owe history a debt. We must see that the land is returned to the Native Americans."

I laughed. Now it was the Indians. Marge insisted she had been one in her last life. She had seen *Dances with Wolves* four times and cried each time. I saw it and laughed. Tame wolves! Sioux warriors that acted like Ghandi!

"I would love to see you tell my father," I told her, "or my grandpa Alistair, that you were giving their ranches back to the Cheyenne or the Crow."

"Don't be cynical, Warren. It will happen because it is just. And when you meet my friends in Pendleton, don't be so aloof and defensive. It messes up everyone's vibes."

"You used to like me when I was withdrawn," I mocked her.

"You were a challenge," she said. "I thought you were dark and mysterious, like a poet. But you're just dark."

"Maybe I am a poet. A Dylan Thomas. Or a Bob Dylan. An Edgar Allen Poe?"

"Still not dark enough," she said. "You are a sociopathic Emily Dickinson. A sentimental romantic who lives in rooms without windows."

"My comfort has been rooms without windows," I snapped. It was a cold, calculated warning. My way of drawing the line. She knew what I meant, and she knew she dare not cross the line.

We drove in silence. My hand on the steering wheel became sweaty and started to ache, and only then did I realize how hard I was gripping it. The Miata handled a tight corner in a river canyon smoothly, like mercury in a glass tube, and as we eased out of the curve, a white

sign on a shadowed hillside stared us in the face. It read:
DO YOU KNOW JESUS AS SAVIOR (JOHN 3:16)? I saw
Marge close her eyes. She refused to look at things she
considered intolerant. Just across the highway from the
sign were two little white crosses. Highway markers for
traffic fatalities. Did they close their eyes too? I wondered.

We found seats in the rodeo grandstands surrounded
by a sea of men and women in western shirts and straw
hats with identically dressed children that screamed a
lot. The air was heavy with the smell of hot dogs, beer,
peanuts, and cigarette smoke.

"Warren," Marge said icily, "I might become ill." She
shuddered and held her pretty little frame tightly. "We
are in a pack of carnivores," she whispered. "I can smell
their collective bad breath, foul with the stench of
rotting flesh."

"That's me," I said. "It's a new cologne. Essence of
Roadkill."

"I'm going to become ill."

"You get sick here," I warned her, "and I get sick at
your space-cadet meeting."

Touché.

The announcer's voice came slickly over the public
address system, welcoming one and all. I imagined him
clean-shaven and ripe with Aqua Velva. The chutes were
so distant he was but a tiny figure elevated above the
arena in the crow's nest. There was a primal, bestial
clamor as the chutes filled with saddle broncs, and I

strained my eyes looking at the stick figures of cowboys trying to find someone who looked like Dickie. They all did. The Grand Entry brought the crowd to its feet as rodeo queens paraded into the dusty arena horseback. Hands were placed over hearts for the singing of the national anthem.

"A typically imperialist ceremony," Marge whispered. When the last rodeo queen rode away, the crowd roared and the Aqua Velva man announced the first section of the saddle bronc riding. A chute gate opened and a stick figure emerged on a big brown horse.

Margie screamed. "It's just like I heard," she cried. "They have a torture device around that poor animal's genitals." The people in the row ahead of us turned and gave us strange looks.

"That's a flank strap," I told her. "It does not go around the genitals."

"Of course it does. It must be Freudian."

"Marge," I said, gripping her arm. "That animal was a gelding. It does not even have genitals."

"Oh, I knew it," she said. "They castrated it with that strap. It will never be free to enjoy sex."

"You know a lot about emasculation," I told her. "But this time you are out of your league."

"I also know a lot about enjoying sex," she retorted. Touché.

"I'm getting sick, Warren."

"Sick? But it's just started," I said. "At the end is the bullriding. That's when things really get bloody."

"Warren . . ." she cupped her hand over her mouth.

"It will be cowboy blood," I said. "The bulls usually win."

"Warren . . ." Her tone was sharper.

I gave in. "OK, go to the car. I want to go behind the chutes. I'll join you in a little while."

I obtained access to the chutes by draping all of Marge's and my cameras around my neck and strutting with a professional arrogance—learned at work—past a security guard. I gave him a condescending nod as I passed.

I approached the dusty, earthy area of the chutes with nervous apprehension. I was a time-traveler stepping through a warp, an alien from another world with a sign around my neck declaring: *I Am Not One of You.*

No one noticed me. The cowboys were boyishly young and consumed by adrenaline-induced concentration. The saddle bronc contestants sat on the ground in their saddles lifting one stirrupped leg at a time, stretching their hamstrings. The bareback riders walked in quiet isolation, their hats pulled down tightly on bent heads, their legs whipping out in exaggerated kicks. The bullriders stared through metal pens at their horned adversaries while they rubbed rosin on their bullropes. They were men about to face danger, possibly death, but they had the nonchalance of office workers.

They did not look like how I remembered or imagined Dickie. They were too young, too clean. They could have been college tennis players or golf pros.

It was too antiseptic, too businesslike. I saw an amiable-looking cowboy standing by himself. He wore no number, spurs, or chaps.

"How many of these cowboys have gone to college?" I asked him.

"Almost all of them," he said. His soft voice was difficult to hear beneath the din of Aqua Velva man's announcements.

"They get scholarships," he continued. "You see that guy, the bullrider? He's got a degree in plant science from Cal-Poly."

"How many are ranch cowboys?" I asked.

"A few of them, but not many. See that bronc rider—he's a world champion. Raised in the suburbs of Dallas. His father was a cop. And that guy"—he pointed to another bullrider—"he was raised in the Bronx."

"The Bronx, New York?"

"Yup. He's white, but there's black guys from the city on the pro circuit."

Black guys. I wondered what Dickie would have thought. The one McColley consistency was a learned racism.

"Where are you from?" I asked.

"Florida."

"What do you do? Are you a bronc rider or what?"

"Naw, man. I'm a pilot. I fly three of these guys from rodeo to rodeo. We hit five, six rodeos a week all over the country."

I thanked him and walked away. It was not Dickie's world. His spirit was not there. These were professional men, more like me than my brother.

I passed through the applauding crowd with its hot dog smells and heard the clamor of chutes, a buzzer, and the Aqua Velva man dim behind me as I entered the parking lot.

Marge was recovered from her social disease—a lack of ease at being with the wrong social group—and seemed glad to see me.

"It got to you too, didn't it?" she said.

"No," I said. "I was too concerned about you."

"You lie." She wanted to drive. It was payback time. Time to visit the weirdos.

"One thing, Warren, about these people we are going to see . . ."

"Yes?"

"I'm not Marge to them, so please don't call me Marge."

"What then, Margaret?"

"No. Shaulitta Starlight. Don't laugh," she warned.

I laughed.

"Sompa gave me the name. It's my spiritual identity. My spiritual guide revealed it to him."

"Who's Sompa? Who's your spiritual guide?"

"Sompa was an Inca warrior. Two thousand years ago. He only comes through the channel of Roger—he is the Master. It is his house we are going to. Spiritual guides are, well, just spiritual entities. Everyone has one."

"So there is Roger and Sompa and some spiritual guide?" I asked.

"Yes, you will only see Roger, but you will hear the voice of Sompa."

"And the spirit guide?"

"You won't see or hear him. Or her. Whatever the case might be."

"It sounds like a strange sort of trinity," I told her.

"Don't get Catholic on me, Warren."

"I wasn't raised Catholic," I reminded her. She was raised Catholic. I was raised a McColley, a confirmed agnostic and materialist with pantheisitic leanings. Actually, when I first met Marge, she was thinking of entering a convent to become a nun. There was something very gothic about her. I could imagine her praying in cold brick sanctuaries, saying her rosaries beneath stained-glass windows and statues of saints, cloistered within rock walls with gargoyles as watchmen. But I couldn't imagine her giving up sex.

It looked like any other house on any street in America, I thought. But it wasn't. It was where the spooks lived. Marge—Shaulitta—knocked.

"If you've never been here," I asked quietly, "how did you know where to come, and how did Sompa give you the name?"

"He sent me a map. I got the name over the telephone."

"He gave you your spiritual name over the phone?"

"Yes. Several of us. A conference call."

"A conference-call seance?"

"Behave yourself, Warren. This man has very high vibes."

Then why does he need a phone? I wondered.

The door opened and Roger filled the entryway. He was an enormous oriental man, the size of a Sumo wrestler, dressed in a colorful robe with layers of chains hanging from his thick neck. "Shaulitta," he said, with a voice as deep as a drum. They embraced warmly and I watched my wife disappear into his mass. Moments later she emerged, as if pulled from a vat, and she seemed different, transformed.

"Master," she said, "this is my earth-mate, Warren McColley." Earth-mate? I extended my hand. She shook her head. "It is vain to offer your right hand," she explained. "It displays your strength, not your weakness."

Roger grinned. "You are a new soul," he said. "I can hug you and greet you with a holy kiss, or we can shake left hands."

I offered my left hand. It vanished in his.

He led us into his house. It was dark, and I noticed the window shades were drawn. A circle of shadows were sitting around a large oak table in the living room. We joined them. There were five of them. Three older women, one older man, a young man who looked like a captured shoe salesman.

"Brothers and sisters," Roger said quietly, "may you greet our sister, Shaulitta Starlight, and her earth-mate, Warren McColley." They nodded wordlessly.

"Has Sompa visited?" Marge—Shaulitta—asked.

"He has promised to," Roger said. He turned to a wrinkled woman with long gray hair. "Have we unity?" he asked. She closed her eyes for several moments. When she looked up I could tell—in spite of the dimness of the room—that she was looking at me.

"There is one slightly discordant vibration," she said.

Roger sighed, and I thought I felt the table quiver. "Well," he said, "I am sure Sompa can overcome any negativity."

I felt Marge's foot nudge my ankle. Quit being negative, she was saying.

We joined hands. I bowed my head as if to pray but noticed the others didn't. They sat straight, eyes closed but heads level. "Think deep, holy thoughts directed toward the Ascended Masters," Roger said. I got the feeling he was coaching me. I closed my eyes and thought about the Trailblazers and who they might pick in the first round of the NBA draft.

Suddenly I sensed a strange energy, almost like electricity but more subtle, moving through my arms. I opened one eye. Roger's massive, fleshy face was going through a range of elastic distortions. His lips became thinner, his face more narrow and ruddy. For a moment I imagined some sort of ceremonial headdress of gold and feathers. Collective thought transferences, I told myself. An illusion caused by deeply felt hopes. Then the lips moved and a high-pitched nasal voice spoke.

"I am Sompa," it said, "guardian of the Inner Circle of the Sun." I felt Marge's hand tingle with excitement.

"There is baseness among you," Mr. Sinus-Problem continued. "I sense a disruption of harmony."

Dang, I thought. He knows I have been thinking that the Trailblazers should trade Duckworth and Kersey. But is that disruptive? No. Now, had I been thinking they should trade Drexler . . .

"Bitterroot," he said.

My mind froze. The room blackened. From my one open eye I glanced at Marge. She seemed light-years removed from me.

"I see white mountain flowers," Sompa continued. "But I do not see mountains. I see plains and prairie. Sheep. I see sheep."

I felt ill to my stomach. Maybe I would become sick, like I had threatened. My forehead was damp but the air in the room felt suddenly cool. I wondered if Marge felt it, but she seemed focused only on the words of the channeller.

Sompa continued: "I see a small house. A little room with one window. A boy. The window seals itself. It is gone. The sheep bleat. The white flowers turn pink with blood."

I saw what he was speaking. I was there again. My grandfather's house. The summer I turned twelve. A scream gurgled in the pit of my stomach. I wanted to stand, break the circle, and have Sompa return to the grave and mind his own bloody business.

The high pitched voice returned: "There has been a transference of blood-crime. There is baseness here. Deception. I must go. I cannot return until the stained vessel is cleansed."

The session was over. I felt discouragement in the circle of hands. Roger's face returned to roundness and the blackness of the room abated. Marge's eyes were still closed, but I sensed her tension and disappointment.

Roger opened his eyes, and the hands of the circle unfolded. "Sompa was defiled," he said. "I fear we have made a grave mistake."

"Will he return?" Marge asked. I had never heard her sound so desperate, not even when we lost her cat at a rest stop in California.

"In time," Roger said. "When, I do not know."

"Is there anything we can do?" Marge asked. *We* meant me.

Roger shrugged his mountainous shoulders. "Perhaps," he said. "Perhaps as a group we can heal psychic wounds."

"We'll do anything," she said.

"What does bitterroot mean?" he asked.

"It is the state flower of Montana," she said.

"Who is from Montana?" he asked.

She glanced at me.

I was sweating. Nothing in six years of college had prepared me for this.

"What is the house with the window?" Roger asked me.

"I don't know," I said. Everyone knew I was lying and waited with placating eyes. Their silence lay on me like a wool blanket on a summer day.

"Your wounds can be healed," Roger implored.

Don't give me that crap, I wanted to shout. I am a psychologist. I am not one of your fruitloop space cadets. But I did not say anything, I could not explain Sompa, but I could not deny him either. They awaited my answer. Finally I said: "I don't know anything about flowers or houses with windows."

"Warren . . ." Marge begged.

"It is OK, Shaulitta Starlight," Roger said. "It must be of his own free will."

I returned to my old friend, *Withdrawal*. I was a rock. Stone-hard cold. Nothing could touch me.

The woman with the wrinkles said to me: "It would be best if the discord did not find root."

Roger nodded. "I am sorry, Shaulitta," he said, "but you and your earth-mate must leave for now."

I arose from the table quickly. Roger followed with my wife, whispering something to her. I felt very alone as if he was more wed to her than I. He bid us good-bye at the door. I sucked fresh air with a new thankfulness. Marge stood coiled in anger.

"How could you?" she demanded.

"How could I what?"

"Denial. You retreated into denial. You lied openly to the group. You disrupted a precious contact with an Ancient One."

"I owe those people nothing," I said.

"You owe me."

I walked to the car. "They are kooks," I told her. "And they were trespassing in my head."

"If they are so kooky," she snapped back, "how did Sompa know the word 'bitterroot,' a word you yourself used just a few weeks ago? How did he know about the house and the window and the boy and the sheep?"

"How do I know?" I shouted. "Maybe he reads minds. Maybe you told him."

"I told him! You think I staged this?"

"Yeah, maybe you did. It's all too important to you."

"You are a fool, Warren. You had a chance not only to have your precarious emotional balance adjusted, but to have your slate cleaned of bad karma."

I laughed. "That Inca dink in the Sumo wrestler's body ain't about to do any wipin' on my slate."

"Do not say ain't. And do not use contractions. You are talking like your family. You are regressing to being a Scottish hillbilly sheepherder."

I nearly slapped her. It was the closest I had ever come to being physical with my wife. "Drop it," I said. "Leave my family out of it. Don't preach emotional healing to me. I'm the psychologist in the family."

"Then heal yourself," she snapped. "The only reason you became a psychologist was to try to figure out your own head."

"And what are you doing becoming some New Age mystic?" I shouted.

"I won't try to explain it to you. You would only analyze me."

"Someone should."

She yelled a profanity at me.

"Good, Marge," I said sarcastically. "Very high vibrations."

She opened the car door, got in, slammed the door, and slumped in the passenger's seat. "You bring out the worst in everyone," she said.

"As a psychologist," I said, "I find that to be a very high compliment."

"Take me home," she said.

"Home? What home? We don't have a home, we have a house. A home has love and laughter and clothes on the floor."

"You wouldn't know," she said.

I roared from the parking space as a last scream of defiance at Sompa, the trespassing blob-god.

We were on Highway 395, a lonely two-lane blacktop. It was night and I soon realized I was driving over eighty miles an hour. The top was still down and Marge had her arms wrapped around her. "I'm freezing," she yelled. "Slow down."

I did the unbelievable. I pushed the pedal to the floor. The cold night air whipped across my face and through my hair. My eyes watered and the drops blew off into the dark. Marge pulled a jacket over her shoulders and huddled forward into the dash. I straightened in my seat, rising above the windshield. Let the wind cleanse me, I screamed in my mind. Let it blow away all the Sompas and Grandpas, all the Rogers and Dickies, all the Marges and Shaulittas. I screamed this again and again in my head, my watering eyes tearing, splashing, and drying. The Miata charged into the darkness, and I rode like a cowboy, a spurring cowboy on the back of a maddened hornet. Hellbent for leather! Yahoo! Powder River, let 'er buck! Divorce, here we come.

Divorce. The spirit hung in the air like the stench of ammonia, like the odor of the blood trail left by Warren's severed soul.

Divorce. Separation. Death. The atmosphere of the room was heavy with the power of darkness.

Marci was being wooed by the soft side of temptation. *Leave him,* the spirit whispered. Amputations often appear to be surgically precise and expedient, but the ghost pains linger for years.

How many times had I considered leaving Donald? Seriously only once or twice, but something in my upbringing, or in my commitment to God's Word, kept me at his side. I was his intercessor. Had Alistair's wife, Isabel, felt that way? Or my mother-in-law or my aunt? Were McColley women anointed to lead lives of gracious martyrdom?

The room became noisier. Perhaps the meal was loosening people up, or maybe others, besides Dick, had had their share from the bar. I sampled my salad and prime rib but pushed the baked potato and creamed corn aside. I did not want to become full. It dulls my senses. Donald sipped his wine and picked at his meal as he polished his speech. I was seated at the end of the head table so there was no one to my left. At least, there wasn't supposed to be.

But suddenly Warren was there.

"Can I interrupt you?" he asked. "Are you finished eating?"

"Interrupt me," I said. After all, it would hardly be the first time. My whole evening had been one interruption after another.

"Reba, I hardly know you. But there's something different about you. Maybe it's just the evening and how it's affecting me, or maybe it was your letter getting me here. I don't know. But you seem like a person who can be trusted."

"Thank you, Warren," I said.

"I know you are religious, but I won't hold that against you." He smiled slyly. I didn't smile back. "It was a joke," he said.

"Oh."

"I have a question that is sort of religious."

"OK."

"Can people come back from the dead?"

"You mean resurrection?" I asked.

"No. Not really. I mean like spirits. Seances. That sort of thing."

"Seances?" I whispered. Donald hadn't even noticed Warren yet, and I certainly did not want him hearing this conversation.

"It's Marge," he said. "She became a channeler. It was part of the problem in our marriage. She took me to see the guru—" Warren paused and glanced past me at Donald. Then he lowered his voice. "This guy claimed to be the voice of some spirit guide named Sompa. He said some really incredible things. Things he shouldn't have known."

"Oh?" I said. "Like what?" I wanted to test the accuracy of my revelations.

He lowered his head in a childlike display of shame. "Things about me and Grandpa. Things about Alistair killing the Big Swede."

"It's demonic," I told him. I wanted to break the heavy yoke of his condemnation.

"Then you believe in demons?" he said, surprised.

"Demonic power is very real."

"So that means you believe in a literal hell?"

"Yes, I do."

"But how did this guy know things that were true?"

"Demons are not omniscient," I explained, "but they do have supernatural intelligence."

"There was a key word. A sort of password."

"What was it?" I asked.

"Bitterroot. The state flower. But they don't even grow around here," he said.

"There is a scripture, I think it is in Hebrews, warning not to allow any bitter root to spring up because many will be defiled."

"None of this is really my area of study," he said.

"It's bad news, Warren. Don't let anything he said influence you."

"I'm not interested. Not in that particular area, anyway."

"There are some good Christian psychologists you can read," I said. "If that would interest you."

"It might. I, well, I'm in a vulnerable spot in my life right now." Warren's pained eyes softened as if he were trying to open a window and let fresh air into his world.

"I will send you some books," I said.

"Thanks, I will read them and mail them back. I will even answer your letters."

"I would enjoy that," I said.

"You wrote to Grandpa?" he said.

"Yes. How did you know?"

"Dick told me. And Grandpa answered?"

"An aide answered for him."

"That's a miracle in itself," he said. "Grandpa actually communicating with people. Maybe people can be raised from the dead."

"All people rise from the dead," I said. "But to different destinations."

"But people don't return from the dead?"

"No, Warren."

"OK, thanks. I will be waiting for the books." He slipped away quietly.

"Reba, I spilled my wine." Donald was dabbing at the table cloth with his napkin. He had never noticed Warren's presence.

"Oh, you didn't get any on you, did you?"

"No," he said. "I don't think so. Can you get me another?"

"But you're about to speak."

"I find it soothing."

"OK," I said. "I'll see what I can do." I had barely left my seat when the house lights went off. It became very dark, and I had to use my hands to guide me. I had been to the portable bar often enough that evening that I was sure I could find it even in the dark. I felt my way, using the smooth backs of chairs to guide me. Surprisingly, the chairs all seemed empty, and I felt alone and exposed. In the thick darkness the only form visible was the faint outline of Pete and Clara silhouetted by the light that glowed on the portrait of Grandpa Alistair.

I felt a cold draft of air pass by me as if I had wandered to an open door. But the chill moved on, leaving no clue to its source.

Then the light at the rostrum came on. *Oh, great,* I thought, *Donald is about to speak.*

Clara and Pete seemed to be staring at the rostrum. There was a motion there. Someone short and bald stepped into the light.

Someone old, short, and bald.

Donald doesn't look too good, I thought.

Then I had to cup a hand over my mouth to stifle a scream.

It was not Donald.

It was Duncan McColley. Clara and Donald's missing father.

12
The Well

Clara? Is that you out there? You're sittin' with *him*, ain't you? Knew ya would be.

You wonderin' where I been? Where I been it's dark, cold, and lonely. Nothin' but memories and mice. I hate the mice, can feel 'em even now chewin' away at my flesh.

Dad-blasted well. I knew you always wanted to use it, Clara. I could tell by the way you'd stand and stare south while we chopped ice on the Slocum pond. Dang well. It was all your ma's idea. Ain't nothin' wrong with choppin' ice. Hard work never hurt a man. But it wasn't just the expense, it was what that well represented.

Twenty years ago I walked into the house cussin' because the ice was so thick on the Slocum pond. Martha was in bed readin' her Bible.

"I've asked you not to swear in this house," she said.

"It's my house," I yelled. "I got a right to swear in it. And I thought I told you I'd have no Bible readin' in this house."

"Only a fool would curse the darkness instead of lighting a candle," she said.

"Whadya mean by that?" I asked.

"Drill a well," she said.

"Too expensive," I said.

"Duncan McColley," she said, "your problem is you prefer the misery of the superficial compared to the price of depth."

I showed her. I ain't afraid of nothin'. I drilled the well. Now I wish I hadn't. I did it for her and she died on me anyway.

Only two things in life ever hurt me. One was you, Clara, marryin' *him*. I know you done it. I know the day you done it. The mice bit particularly hard that day. The other was Martha dyin'. She died before we ever used the well.

You all wanna know what happened to me? Do you wanna know, Donald, or would you rather I go away so you can stand in the spotlight? Well, I'm gonna tell ya what happened.

Sometimes a man gets a feelin' that things ain't right. I had that feelin' that day. I found those ol' cows right where I knew they'd be. I got out and shook the grain bucket at 'em, and they lined-out and began to follow me out of there. It was slow goin'. I had to stop the truck and tease 'em with feed every little ways. But I wasn't in no rush. The weatherman said the storm wasn't due till midnight.

He was wrong. Wind got to really howlin' 'bout three, then the snow started. The jeep trail blew shut. I buried the pickup in a snowbank about five. It was gettin' good and dark by then. I tried to shovel my way out but the wind kept blowin' the snow back as fast as I shoveled. Chill factor musta been a hundred below. The cows turned their tails and left me. I figured I could walk out. Done it many times before.

I shoulda stayed with the truck. That's what I always told you kids. But like I said, it was just one of those days. Mercy, it was cold. I tried climbin' the jeep trail but the drifts were waist-deep. I began to play out. The wind was smackin' me in the face. A lesser man would have laid down and died, I suppose.

It was plumb dark and I lost my bearin's, but I kept climbin', though I was a'feared of fallin' and breakin' a hip. You hear about old geezers doin' that. Finally I was all but crawlin' up that hill, but I made it to the top. The wind was really blowin' up there.

I knew Clara would be lookin' for me. The drivin' snow kept stingin' my face so it was hard to keep my eyes open to look for headlights. Thought I saw some once, but then they were gone. I figured it was just my mind playin' tricks on me. Oh, I got tired. I knew if I ever fell down, I'd never get up. Then I thought I saw Clara. She was just a dim outline in front of me. I yelled, but the words blew back in my face. I spurred myself on. There was Clara, I thought, kinda tall and skinny. Then I bumped into her and it wasn't her at all. It was that durn power pole. I was on the wrong end of the ranch. I was at the well.

Well, old man, you've sure done it this time, I told myself. I knew I didn't have the strength to make it home. Then I remembered the wellhouse. The wellhouse ain't nothin' but a big culvert set down in the ground with a steel lid on top. Ain't much in 'em except wiring to the pump, a pressure tank, and sometimes an electric outlet and a space heater for thawin' out pipes. And mice nests. Always lots of mice nests.

I kicked around the snow till I found the lid. Took all my strength but I got the lid off, climbed down the ladder, and pulled the lid back over me. My, but it seemed warm down there in comparison. Real homey. There was even a lightbulb in the electrical outlet. I plugged it in and it weren't long before I was able to take my gloves off and light me a cigarette.

It weren't bad down in that hole. Fact is, I smoked me a half dozen cigarettes before it dawned on me that somethin' was wrong. I was gettin' giddy-like. Check the lid on this mousetrap, you old fool, I told myself, it could be driftin' over with snow and sealin' out the air. I climbed up the ladder and tried to crack the lid a little, but couldn't. I was just weak, I figured, and would rest a little and try again. I cussed myself for ever climbin' down in that hole. Now it looked like I was stuck. Guess you could call it Martha's revenge.

I had me another cigarette. Clara was always gettin' on me to quit. Donald never cared. He figured the sooner I died the sooner he might get the place. After a smoke, I climbed up and tried the lid again. It was stuck worse than before. I knew the snow had drifted over it good. So I pushed real hard and lost my balance, came tumblin' down, strikin' the lightbulb as I fell. I heard it hit the concrete floor and shatter into little flakes like ice. There went my light. I was bruised and sore by the fall but nothin' was broken and outside of it bein' dark I was passably comfortable. Had another smoke though I knew I'd use up more oxygen. I figured everyone had been right: smokin' would kill me.

My only hope for rescue was Clara to think of checkin' the well. But what would make her do that? For a second I thought about prayin'. But that made me laugh, and I cussed the God that Martha had believed in. We McColleys always got the last laugh, I figured.

I'm gonna die in a mouse nest, I told myself. Ain't that a heck of a note? It made me remember the winter my brother Roland and I slept in the haystack. It was the year of the influenza. Our two little sisters, Isabelle and Maybelle, got real sick. To keep us safe Pa made me and Roland sleep outside in the hay covered by a tarpaulin and cowhides. We huddled together, shiverin' at thirty below.

One night I told Roland: "Ma says we should pray for the girls."

"Pa doesn't believe in prayin'," Roland told me.

"But Ma does."

"She's a woman. Women don't know. Besides, the girls are gonna die."

"How come?"

"Cuz Pa told me so. He said they were too weak to live."

So I didn't pray. I shivered. Pa said it would make us tough. Anyway, Roland was right. The girls died.

Bein' in that hole reminded me of that. Everythin' bein' dark and quiet. No one to talk to 'cept the mice.

I kept gettin' more and more light-headed. At one point I thought I saw the lid open. I gave a little whimper of joy as I saw a skinny old man climbin' down the ladder. He wasn't dressed for the cold at all and was packin' somethin' heavy in his arms.

Then I realized it was my pa, ol' Alistair.

He misstepped on the last rung of the ladder and tumbled and fell in a heap beside me. The tin box he was carryin' must have been heavy 'cuz it made a terrible noise as it struck the ground. Ol' Alistair hooted with pain and grasped at his ankle. I could tell it was broken for sure. I knew I was seein' things. I knew this wasn't real, I wasn't that far gone.

"You ain't here," I told him. "You are in a nursin' home in Yellow Rock." The next thing I knowed he was usin' a knife to scrape a hole outa the ground. A hole big enough for his tin box. Lucky for him the diggin' was easy. Then he wrestled that big tin box into the hole. It had some writin' on the lid. But it was too dark for me to read. Somethin' about "Mother." Alistair covered the box up real neat-like, then crawled one-legged back up the ladder. "You sure were a tough sonuvagun," I told him. He paused and looked down as if he was seein' somethin' or maybe not seein' anything at all. Then he pulled himself out, closed the lid, and was gone.

It was lonely when he left. My head was spinnin' and my lungs were burnin' for air. But there wasn't any air to be had.

I started screamin' for Pa to come back. I was screamin' but I wasn't hearin' any words. It seemed like all my pleas were bein' sucked down a long, deep drain. I scratched around where I saw him diggin'. It was dark and I was weak, but there was sure enough somethin' there. I lit a match and looked real close. It was the top of a rusty old tin box. I could barely make out the words *Mother's Love* and the paintin' of a woman, but most of the paint had chipped off so it didn't really look like a woman anymore.

That was my last match. Darkness settled in thick and heavy and squeezed me around the neck. My lungs burned. My body shook and gasped, then it settled back soft and easy like I was home in my rocker. I guess that is when I died. Odd part is, that is when I seemed to come awake. I could feel and see things I never seen before. Fearful things. I mean, my most personal fears sprung alive and scurried over me like mice, bitin' wherever they could get their teeth into my flesh. A terrible, nameless dread began pullin' me downward. I felt like a little spider bein' sucked down a bathtub drain.

Then I heard a sweepin' and scrapin' sound above me. Someone was movin' the wellhouse lid. The dread told me that my greatest fear was comin' to see me. I actually heard somethin' say it: "Prepare for the sum of your fears."

I don't fear nothin', I wanted to say. But that wasn't true. I was afeared old Alistair would come back. I was afeared that the God I didn't believe in might come callin'. I was afeared there were mice as big as grizzly bears comin' to pick my bones clean.

The lid was pulled off. There was now light in the hole. My greatest fear crawled over the edge and dropped down beside me. It was too big to be Alistair. And sure enough not what I expected to be God. It was all bundled up in winter clothes and looked closer to bein' a bear-sized mouse. But it wasn't.

It was Pete Andraxie.

I jumped to attack him. I saw myself rainin' blows down like hail, but he did nothin'. I shuddered at his touch as he removed his glove and put his hand on my neck lookin' for a pulse. I heard him say: "Well, old man, I guess you've cashed in your chips."

A raw, violent energy boiled within me, percolatin' and overflowin' until I threw a mighty punch at his jaw but my fist passed through beard stubble, flesh, and bone as if the man was nothin' but air.

I hated his face. The weak, jaundiced eyes, the fleshy cheeks pink from the cold and puffy from drink. *Leave me alone*, I screamed. *My tomb is private.*

"Remember the hotel room in Hell's Bend?" he asked. "Remember how you told me to just be quiet and lie still. Well, I guess it's your turn to be quiet and lie still." He squatted on his haunches beside me. I could hear the tinkle of spur rowels as he moved, I remembered brandin's where he drank and staggered as a child and my wife took him aside and comforted him. Jealous of the attention he received from Martha and Clara. Attention for nothin' but bein' weak.

"So what do I do with you, old man?" he asked. "Haul you back for a proper burial, or leave you here for the mice?"

Keep your filthy hands off me, I screamed.

"What happens if I take you home?" he asked. "You don't have a will, do you, old man? You figured you'd take it with you. But you can't. Hearses don't have trailer hitches."

He thought I was dead but I never felt more alive. Passionately, violently alive. A throbbin' pulse of hot blood pounded through my veins. I could feel my face flush with anger.

"What was it about me you hated so much?" he asked. "And why were you always standin' in the way of me and Clara? Was it just the booze? If it was, I don't blame you. Clara deserves better than to be hitched to a drunk. But she deserved better than you too."

I screamed. I screamed so loud the echoes swirled like a tornado and flung me against the sides of the wellhouse. But he sat there unruffled, just inches from my cold, blue face.

"The funny thing is," he said, "I'd be dead by now if it weren't for your women. First of all, it was your wife, Martha. She cared for me when everyone else laughed. I felt love from her hands that I never felt since. And Clara has given me reason to live. She sees the good in me, what little there may be. So I guess I owe you a debt, Duncan McColley."

Owe me a debt! A geyser of hot, sulfuric curses spewed from my mouth only to fall back on me, burnin' tiny holes through my clothes. I could smell the stench of burnin' flesh. A growl rose from my belly at him in a voice that echoed in my bones. *Don't talk about McColley women and their prayers. Don't afflict me with your pitiful gratitudes.*

"Yeah, I owe you a debt," he said. "I thank you for your women, but what do I do with you, Duncan McColley?"

He pressed my eyelids closed, but I could still see. He positioned my cold, stiff corpse to appear comfortable and covered my face with my cap. "Funny thing is," he said, "everyone knows you hate this well. No one's gonna look down here."

Then how did you find me, Pete Andraxie?

"Can't say what led me here," he said. "Don't know why you hated the well so much either. Was it too expensive?"

Expensive! Yes, it was expensive. It cost me my pride.

As I mentioned pride, my soul began a long freefall into a cold, dark canyon where snarlin' packs of starvin' coyotes fought over my flesh while mice ran through the portals of my ribs. The canyon was steep and stony as if I had dropped to the center of the earth. The wellhouse was high above me and the echoes of Pete Andraxie's words fell like little pebbles.

"Money was never the problem, was it?" I heard Pete Andraxie say. "It was control. You just had to control people."

I was my father's son! I yelled. But my voice was drowned out by the howls of the red-eyed predators that formed the darkness I dwelt in.

"The wind's blowin'," Pete said. "The snow will cover my tracks. No one will know I was here."

I will know, I shouted and felt my words rise with the cry of the pack.

"You will lie still and be quiet," Pete said. "I need time to think this through. I'll take care of Clara."

Clara was his. I rose to my feet, flesh hangin' in ribbons from my limbs. I began climbin' the wall. I was back in the well just as Pete turned to leave. His eyes caught the soft glint of light reflectin' off the lid of the old tin box. "What's this?" he said, and he brushed his boot across the cover revealin' the chipped face of a painted woman and the words *Mother's Love* illuminated above her like a halo. I crawled from the abyss, draggin' the hounds of hell with me. *The gold is mine!* I screamed, and I rolled across the box to cover it from his sight. His boot moved right through me.

"Just some junk," he said. "Your grave is a garbage pile, Mr. McColley." Then he crawled up the ladder and closed the lid behind him. I hated to see him go. I was lonelier yet, but even worse, I needed Pete Andraxie. I needed someone to hate. I am settled only in knowin' he must someday return, and for this I wait.

My days are spent now scratchin', diggin', and clawin'. Scratchin' and diggin', not to claw free from my wellhouse grave, but to uncover the box, to rip the lid from *Mother's Love* and count the treasure within.

It is cold, lonely, and dark where I dwell. The hounds of hell are gone, having stripped me bare. The mice hardly torment me at all. It is cold, lonely, and dark in the bottom of this well, but the treasure of Alistair Angus McColley is mine.

He was gone as mysteriously as he had appeared. Or had I seen him at all? I was frozen in shock. I could feel my heart beating and the strain of my eyes trying to focus in the dark. But I could not move. The light now shone on an empty dais.

I had just heard someone speak from the dead. I knew where the body of Duncan McColley, my father-in-law, lay. I was overwhelmed with pity for the man. He and I had never been close. Duncan had taken little interest in me or his grandchildren. Ten dollars for each of us at Christmas, that was what I remembered of Duncan McColley.

Along with pity for Duncan, I felt fear. There was an evil presence in the room. Or was this all in my mind? Was I in fact experiencing a complete mental breakdown? I prayed softly and fervently under my breath. I prayed for protection.

I had to find Marci. Marci had been right. We needed to get away from the room and pray.

The shock wore off. The paralysis left me, but the room was still dark and silent. I could no longer see the shadowed outlines of Pete and Clara. I felt alone. My groping hands touched the cool, smooth surfaces of chairs, tables, and plates. I did not think about Donald.

My thoughts turned completely to Marci. I needed her fellowship. I needed someone who represented Christ.

I moved slowly, breathing with deliberation as if in labor. Ahead of me I saw an outline of Dick's black hat. And I could make out the form of Marci sitting beside him.

"Marci," I whispered. "Can you hear me?"

Then a cold draft passed by me again and this time I did not mistake it for a draft from a door. It was alive.

I turned and looked back at the dais. There was motion in the light as if the air particles were vibrating to fight off an invader. A darkness moved in and a form stepped into the light. Another small, wiry, bald-headed old man. My knees weakened and I felt faint. Only an inner strength kept me standing; for whatever reason, I was to witness this. I was not to escape by fainting.

The figure at the dais turned and looked at me. He stood where only moments before I had imagined Duncan McColley standing. He seemed perched on the dais, angry and arrogant, his breath swelling in his jutted chest like a cock about to crow.

It was the Rooster. Roland McColley.

13
Endless Radio

I'm not really here, you know. I'm a ghost. But I am gonna tell you where I am, so that you might know.
I died of a heart attack last winter while in the hills feedin' cows with my son, Dickie.

I remember a brief sleeplike time, like takin' a nap after the noon meal, snoozin' off while listenin' to Paul Harvey on the radio. I flew in my dreams through a darkness formed like a great thunderstorm with lightnin' flashin' on all sides of me. I came down through the clouds, undampened by the gray drizzle of rain. The land was bleak and brown and dotted with whirlwinds. Dust devils. Thin cattle stood forlornly by the banks of dry streams. Nothin' seemed to grow but weeds. The ol' country was a lot drier than I remembered it.

Below me a pickup was parked at a reservoir. Before fallin' asleep, I was at that reservoir. Only it had been winter, and Dickie was breakin' ice. I was reachin' for the shovel. But now it wasn't winter anymore, it seemed to be the dead of summer. I came down out of the sky like a feather, through the roof of the four-wheel drive and into the driver's seat. I looked for Dickie, but he wasn't there. I tried turnin' the radio on. My hands missed the dial as if I was in a dream. I couldn't get a grip. But I persisted until I succeeded. The announcer said the day was gonna be hot and dry.

I had trouble grippin' the steerin' wheel too. My hands passed through it. But the more I concentrated and cursed, the more solid it became until finally I got a grip on it. The best I could tell it was midday. An orange, shadowed sun hung high in the gray sky. Fires were burnin' somewhere and leavin' a canopy of smoke. The brown and black hills were outlined with red.

Where's Dick? I wondered, and I looked toward the slimy, boilin' moss-filled pond. I watched moisture rise in the air and evaporate before my eyes. A rusty ax with a splintered handle lay on the bank.

"Dickie," I yelled, but my voice echoed in the cab of the truck, bouncin' from one corner to another like an agitated housefly.

"Dickie is not here," the radio said.

I was hearin' things. I played with the dial until I found another station.

"Good morning," the announcer said.

What's so good about it? I wondered, but I was glad to hear a friendly voice.

"Today is June 1, 1956. In our birth announcements for today, a son was born to Roland and Sarah
McColley. He was christened Richard Roland
McColley and weighed seven pounds and six ounces.
Big boy for a McColley. He is destined to grow taller
than his father, have a good outside jump shot, will
drift from job to job most of his life, and will eventually
murder his father by placing a shovel just out of the
old man's reach."

What? I thought. *I'm hearin' things again.* I fingered
the knobs, but my hand passed through the radio until
I cursed it solid. This time I got a familiar station, one
with weather and cattle market reports. Murder his
father? Who would say that?

I thought I knew where I was, but I wasn't sure. There
were tracks in the pasture road in front of me. Red
tracks in black dust. If I followed the tracks, I knew the
road would take me home. Dickie would be home, with
what's her name, his wife. The pickup chugged and
bucked, but I got it onto the trail where it settled into
tracks like a train on a rail.

"And here is your midsessions report," the radio said.
"On the Chicago Mercantile, cattle futures opened at
their lowest level in years and are already at the limit—
down in heavy trading. Prolonged drought and con-
sumer resistance to red meat has further softened a
weak market. Severe drought lingers in Montana and
long-range forecasts see no relief in sight."

Drought. Poor cattle prices. How would I ever pay
the bills? I felt sick to my stomach and screamed a long

list of profanities at the radio. The more I screamed the
louder the radio became.

"In other news, funeral services will be held today for
area resident, Roland Angus McColley, son of pioneer
Montana sheepman Alistair Angus McColley. Services
will be at the family ranch. Pallbearers will be needed,
two or three will do, as Mr. McColley was not very
heavy."

"Liar!" I yelled. "I ain't dead, and I've got friends
enough to carry me."

I turned it off. What kind of joke was this? Dickie
was behind it all, I knew that. Always a joker. That stunt
he'd pulled on that black man had got the whole town
to laughin'. But I was never much for jokes, and I didn't
care for this one. How had he done it? How had he
rigged the radio? I braked the truck, got out, and walked
around it, lookin' for Dickie, lookin' for tape recorders
or wires or some evidence of a prank. I found nothin'.
It was stiflin' hot. I needed water but didn't have any.
I drove on, raisin' a rooster tail of black dust behind me.

A barbed-wire fence stopped me. The fence was eight
wires high. *What's this for?* I wondered. This had been
a four-wire fence before. I waited in the truck for Dickie
to get the gate, then I remembered he wasn't there. I
had to open the gates myself.

I got out and put a shoulder into the gate-post. I
pushed with all my strength but couldn't get the gate to
budge. *Why did he have to go and build this gate so tight?* I
wondered. I went back to the truck to look for some
fencin' pliers but couldn't find any. Just like Dickie,

always losin' things. Well, I'd just unwrap the wires by hand. The fence glowed blue like it was charged, but I knew it wasn't. We were too far from electricity and batteries just go dead. So I grabbed the wires and shock lifted me into the air and threw me backwards like I was a sack of air. I landed on the hood of the truck but it didn't hurt me any.

Now why did he go and electrify this fence? I wondered. That boy would sure have some explainin' to do.

I couldn't open the gate and I couldn't crawl through the wires. There wasn't nothin' I could do 'cept get back in the truck and find another gate.

The radio came on by itself.

"In local news, pioneer stockman Alistair Angus McColley has been found guilty of the murder of Karl Hannson, better known as the Big Swede. The jury ruled that McColley acted with deliberate vengeance in striking Mr. Hannson in the head with a shovel. The judge has sentenced McColley to be hanged. The execution will be carried out this evening on Main Street here in Yellow Rock. Tickets for the hanging can be . . ."

"That's a lie!" I screamed. "Pa was found innocent. It was self-defense." My blood was boilin' within me. I had to get to Yellow Rock in time to stop the hangin'. I rammed the truck into gear and began drivin' as fast as I could. I hit some terrible bumps and washouts. At one point, in my mirror I saw Dickie fly out and land on his back. So there's Dickie, I thought. He's been ridin' in the back all this time. But I couldn't stop. I had to get to Yellow Rock.

It seemed like I drove for hours. I drove so long that time lost meanin'. But I could not find a gate I could open, and everywhere the fences were eight wires stretched tighter than banjo strings. *I never knew Dickie to care much for fencin',* I thought, *but who else could have done it?*

My neighbors? Had they conspired to fence me in? I was suspicious and angry. I could understand takin' a shovel to someone's head.

On I drove. Cattle stared at me as I went by, their eyes bloodshot with dust and pleadin' for feed or water. I saw carcasses bloated with death, the outline of my brand stretched large and tight against the skin. I had never seen the range look this bad. Not even in '34 or '61 or '88.

I must be gettin' old, I thought, cuz I can't find my way home. The radio played constantly. I kept turnin' the dial. I was tired of hearin' about drought and bad cattle prices.

I picked up a high school basketball game: " . . . The ball is passed to McColley in the corner. He squares up, releases a soft, floating jumper. It ripples the net. Dick McColley now has twenty-two points for Yellow Rock High . . ."

What's he doin' playin' ball? I wondered. He should be workin'. He should be out lookin' for me.

"McColley is the top college prospect in the state," I heard the announcer say. "But his father has never seen him play."

"There's more to life than basketball!" I shouted.

"There's more to life than land and cattle," the announcer said.

Quit talkin' about me, I snapped back. Tell Dickie to get out here and lead me home. But the announcers now were silent.

I turned the dial. I was weary with a strange tiredness. My muscles didn't ache. I just felt lifeless. I kept comin' to the same gates and was weaker at each gate. And each gate seemed tighter, higher, and more electrified.

Wherever I was, I was stayin'. The land became darker, more desolate as I drove. It has the feel of a terrible dream yet was more real than anything I had ever experienced. I felt like I was a figment of my own imagination.

"In local news, Alistair Angus McColley, pioneer Yellow Rock area stockgrower, was hanged by his neck until dead this evening for the murder of Karl Hannson, the Big Swede. The jury was unanimous on the murder charge following the testimony of the prosecution's chief witness, Alistair McColley's grandson, Warren McColley."

"No," I spat, "it's all a lie and you know it. Pa ain't dead. He never committed no crime. Warren froze up on the stand. He never said nothin', he just sat there and sobbed and cried until the lawyer led him away." It was all lies. I was surrounded by lies. I hit the radio with my fist. I hit it again and again and again but I might as well have been strikin' a rock wall with pillows.

The radio crackled and changed stations on its own.

"Warren McColley, valedictorian of the Yellow Rock High School Class of 1972 has left home . . ." Crackle. Crackle.

"It is appointed once unto man to die, and then judgment."

A gospel station. I hate gospel stations. I spewed a cloud of curses, and the radio hissed with static and the stations blurred one voice into another. Rock-and-roll, country, NPR. They all played songs about me and my life.

Fear flowed in my veins. I sucked for air like a fish out of water. My heart beat fiercely, making my ribs ache.

Fight harder, I told myself. *Resist this. It is all a dream.*

I drove on. There seemed no end to the gasoline in my tank. The land kept unfoldin' in front of me like book page after book page. Vultures perched on scoria-tipped buttes squawked and took wing as I drove by. They followed me.

Fires burned in the distance. The horizon glowed red with flames. I drove across miles and miles of my best pastureland scorched like charcoal and dotted with the burnished skeletons of cattle and deer. The air was congested by smoke, dust, and smolderin' flesh. The only thing alive were the weeds. Canadian thistle, leafy spurge, knapweed. They seemed to be sowed and cultivated by my passin'.

I turned onto a jeep trail that climbed a high divide. For a moment the weather—in fact, the entire season—changed and it was winter. It began snowin'. The temperature dropped drastically. *What a freak storm,* I thought as I turned the heater on. Ahead of me I saw a vehicle stuck in the snow. It looked like my brother's truck. What was Duncan doin' here? But as I approached, the truck was gone, the snow stopped, and I climbed to a high pass in the hills and into another land. The weather warmed. I could actually feel the sun radiatin' off the hood of the truck. I dropped down to green, grassy meadows grazed by fat cattle wearin' my brand. Grass. I was finally in grass. There were cattle and sheep grazin' contently on a thousand hills.

" ... It was a record day on the Chicago Merc," the radio announcer said, "as cattle futures hit new highs ..."

I was ecstatic. The bad dream had ended. Somehow I had crossed over to the desires of my heart. Everythin' I ever wanted: fat cattle, money, and there—just past the four-wired fence—sat my house. Dickie would be there. I got out to open the gate, invigorated with relief. Near the gate, a tin box sat half-buried in the ground. It was an old-fashioned tin, the kind used to store foodstuffs. Alistair used to keep tins like these, I remembered. On the lid was the face of a smilin' woman and the words Mother's Love Baking Powder. I pried the lid off. Inside the box glowed with bars and coins of solid gold. Alistair's buried fortune. My father had left it for me. I reached in to claim my fortune, but the gold became chalky in my hands and turned to coal. A blast of hot, gritty wind hit me in the face and the grass withered before my eyes, the cattle thinned to hairless skeletons that collapsed in heaps and the fence glowed blue and impassable. The home on the creek faded to a rottin' homesteader's shack and vanished in a sea of heat waves. It had all been an illusion.

I crawled back into the truck.

" . . . Condemned to wander dry and waterless places," I heard the radio say.

I was angry and afraid, but my strongest sense was one of separation. I was alone. But what of that? I had always been a loner, even as a husband and a father. I had been content with my own company. Now I felt detatched, but detatched from what?

I was lonely. No Dickie. No Warren. No Alistair. I had no one to share my sufferin'. And yet, I wasn't totally alone because of the radio. Endless noise, endless voices. One voice seemed to be comin' through clearer than the others, and it was sayin' somethin' about church and Jesus.

"Shut up, shut up!" I yelled. "You know I hate listenin' to preachers on the radio."

"But, Roland, you won't let me go to church. The only time I get inside a church anymore is for a wedding or a funeral. I swear, the next time will probably be my own . . ."

Sarah? My wife?

"Sarah!" I screamed.

Crackle. ". . . Funeral services were held today for Sarah Erskine McColley, wife of Roland McColley . . ."

"Sarah!"

Crackle. ". . . And the righteous shall be raised to everlasting glory, but the wicked to eternal punishment . . ."

"Sarah!"

Crackle. "I don't believe in God. I don't believe in religion. I don't want you wastin' your time goin' to church and cacklin' with those other ol' hens and those limp-wristed, milquetoast preachers . . ."

My voice. I was listenin' to my voice.

". . . If God is so big and so good, why don't it rain? I ain't afraid of hell. I will carve my own little empire out of it. The devil ain't tangled with no one until he's messed with Roland 'the Rooster' McColley. My pa taught me I could spit in Satan's eye if I had a mind to . . ."

I cursed the radio to change stations but only found my own voice again.

". . . If Warren wants to leave, let him leave. I don't care. Dickie wants to join the Marines. Let him. I brought 'em into the world, now they can fend for themselves."

"Shut off!" I yelled. "Shut off." But the radio kept playin'. " . . . For God so loved the world that He sent His only Son . . ."

Suddenly I was blindsided by truth. It did not come as an idea, a revelation in my own head. It came as a force with a power of its own. It washed through me like soft warm oil and found me wantin'. I felt contaminated, not only by its presence, but by what its presence revealed about me. I had an absence. But then, mercifully, it passed on and my hardness resumed its strength.

"I did not know!" I said and waited for the radio to answer.

"You knew. How many friends did you bury, Roland McColley? How many funeral services did you sit through and hear the Word about death and resurrection?"

"But I didn't hear."

"Nor did you hear your wife, your sister-in-law, or your mother."

The terrible agony of separation took form beside me. Loneliness would now be my only companion. I could see it sittin' in the pickup, where Dickie had always sat, and it turned its hideous head and smiled.

"Let me go back," I cried. "Let me tell Dickie and Warren. I don't want them here."

"Would they receive one raised from the dead?" the radio asked.

"Let me go back."

And that is why I am here. That is my story. I have come to you from a dry and thirsty land. Once in it, there is no escape. The gates are all closed. The road leads nowhere. And the radio plays endlessly.

The Rooster was gone. One moment he was speaking to the crowd, the next he merely stepped backward and faded into the darkness. The room seemed blacker with the exception of the light that shone on the portrait of Alistair Angus McColley. It seemed to glow with a life of its own.

I forgot about Marci. I needed Donald. I needed my stern, practical, unspiritual husband. He would tell me that nothing unusual had happened, to quit being silly, to grow up and stop being so super-spiritual. Donald, my anchor.

I told my body to move, but it wouldn't. I felt panic rising from my belly, reaching for my heart.

Then I felt peace. A sudden, overpowering, unexpected peace.

"Lord," I whispered. "Are you in this?" I heard no answer, but the peace seemed to deepen and spread. I could move now. I felt my way slowly toward the light at the podium. That is where I would find my Donald. I saw a hand extend into the vector of light illuminating a gold wedding band. It was my hand. I had reached the dais. "Donald," I whispered.

I was aware of closeness. A bald head with a friendly smiling face formed in the light.

"Donald?" I asked.

"No, Reba," the face said. "It's me. Alistair Angus McColley."

14
Borderlands, Lowlands, Highlands

I awoke to the sweet scent o' grass, as familiar as the heather o' me 'omeland, and a kaleidoscope o' flowers includin' rhododendrons as red and purple as a Montana sunset. The sky was bluish in twilight with no sight o' either sun or moon. I was content to lie for several minutes absorbin' the healin' richness o' the soil and balmy perfume o' the fauna. There was moisture in the air as maybe a wee smear of rain had passed through by me earthen bed, but me clothes were dry.

Aye, Alistair, I told myself, *wherever ye be 'tis far removed from the nursin' home.* And glad o' it, I was. I took a deep breath and sucked in the perfume of the land. I felt cleansed from the sterile stink o' the rest home, the pungent odors of urine and disinfectant, and yet, I could not smell the salty sea. I surely expected to smell the sea.

In due time, I rose to my feet and was surprised by the ease o' that activity. Me muscles should have been weak and stiff from years o' ridin' a bed, but I uncoiled like a young-un and stood in the jeweled dusk of the evenin'. Wherever I was they was havin' a gid year. The grass was green and knee-high. It waved softly in the breeze. The trees were full-limbed and shaggy with leaves. The air was warm, but the sheepherder in me was wary. Build a fire, I thought, but the pockets of me clothin' were devoid of matches or anythin' else for that matter. How I had come to journey from the nursin' home to this fine pasture I hadn't a clue, yet I was peaceful and wanted only one thing, the warmth and assurance of fire, for I did not know what the night would bring.

Where was I? Aye, it had to be the Old Country, me 'ome, the Ciogach district o' Lochbroom, on the seaward side o' Ben Moor o' the Mists. Scotland. Me Scotland. How I had arrived and who had brought me I did not know and I did not care.

Darkness never really fell. It had to be summer, the season o' the midnight sun. Yet, it darkened jest enough for me to detect a faint glow risin' o'er a distant knoll. I walked to it, testin' me muscles as if I were a bairn.

I was astonished by what I saw. I took it to be a spray o' water at first. A fountain eruptin' from the ground like a fluorescent geyser. But as I neared, it was plain it weren't water a-tall, but fire. I had never seen the like o' it. A broken gas main, I figured, but there was no sign o' industry thereabouts, and the fire was not a-roarin' as a gas fire does. It made nary a noise a-tall. And yet, daur I say it, it seemed to have a life of its own. I backed away, not in fear, but in respect.

I returned to the heather and settled in to await whoever it was I was expectin'. I examined me clothin', trousers and tunic. They were as soft and white as lamb's fleece and every bit as comfortin'.

I tried to remember where I had come from, but me recollections were sparse, just snatches o' black and white scenes from a world that seemed far, far away. Yellow Rock, Montana, was a name, but I could put no faces to the title. The smell o' sickness, the frailty of me body, those memories were dimmin' with each moment as if purged by the perfume o' the meadow. I had been old, sick, and angry, and now I was not. At least, I did not feel that way.

Someone had brought me 'ome to Scotland, and whoever that was, they would be back. I felt great expectations of an imminent arrival. I had fallen asleep and they had left me in peace. They would be back shortly. My patience amazed me. It was not a quality I was known for.

The night blued to a velvet purple but blackness never came. Suddenly I became aware of a presence. A few yards from me sat a person. My companion had returned.

"Yah, Alistair," he said, "it is a good night, is it not?"

"Aye, it is," I said. "Very good."

"Pardon me for bein' so slow in comin'." The voice was deep and husky as if risin' from a deep well. "I am not much of a herder anymore. Never was, I suppose."

I could not see the man. He was only a large outline leanin' 'gainst the trunk of a tree. "Aye, man," I said. "You brought me to this place, did you not?"

"Brought you? Oh, mercy no. No one brought you. Not directly anyway, though some were sure to have helped. But you came alone. Everyone does, you know."

No. I did not know. So I asked: "Where am I exactly?"

"This is called the Borderlands," my companion said.

"The Borderlands," said I. "Then it is true. I am 'ome."

"You are home," said the man. "But you won't stay here. I have brought with me a small flock of sheep; you must herd them beyond here."

"Herd them? Me? To where?"

"Out of the Borderlands, into the Lowlands, and finally to the Highlands." His slight accent jogged vague recollections.

Oh gracious, I thought, a long hard journey across the rugged isle o' Scotland. I did not know if I was up to it. I was accustomed still to bedsheets and bedpans.

He sensed me apprehension. "The journey will take some doing, but the way is not arduous. Fact is, you'll find it enjoyable," he said.

"But the Highlands," I said. "I have not walked the Highlands since me bonnie days o' boyhood when I had the scrap and bounce of a billy goat."

"You have never walked these Highlands," the man said, his voice growing more hauntingly familiar.

"Do I know ye?" I asked.

"Oh, yes, Alistair. Or at least you did."

"Then pray, man, what is your name?" I asked.

"Ahh, you best sleep first," he said. "The morning light will show you my face, and you will have no need to ask of my name."

And, with a surprising lack of curiosity, I stretched out onto the grass with peace as me only blanket and slept the sleep of a young-un.

I awakened to a magnificent sky draped overhead like a turquoise canopy, yet still no sight of the sun. Beside me was a woven basket filled with fruit.

"Good morn to ya, Alistair," said my host. His craggy face was lit by bright blue eyes. He had a mane of wavy blonde hair. I feared for me life.

"Sleep well?" he asked.

"Aye," I said, for I had. I looked about me for a weapon. A tree limb, a rock, anythin'. There was nothin' within reach.

"Ah, you recognize me, Alistair?" the man asked.

"Karl Hannson," I said. The Big Swede.

"It is me, Alistair," he smiled.

"But you are dead," I said.

"Yah, some would say so."

So it is all a trick, I thought. I had been lured somewhere, kidnapped by a descendent of the Big Swede. An eye for an eye. A clansman's revenge. He seemed to know me thoughts.

"You chust don't geet it, do ye, Alistair? Ah, youse always a stubborn one."

"Swedes should not lecture Scots on stubbornness," I told him.

"Yah, that is true," he smiled.

"Kill me if you must," I told him. "I surely have it comin'. Just don't talk me to death."

He laughed a deep, cavernous chuckle. "Oh, Alistair, you are a greenhorn in the Borderlands or you would never say such a thing. Dontcha know where ye be, man?"

"In the Borderlands," I said. "Some kilos north of England."

He laughed louder. "Oh, many kilos north of England I would say."

"Who are ye really?" I asked. "A grandson o' the Big Swede, is that it?" I was still lookin' for the proper weapon, but the trees displayed no dead branches and the ground was without rocks.

"I am who you say I am."

I rose to my feet, my body more supple and stronger than the day before. All about me was a green blaze of glorious grasses and flowers o' every color. "There are no thistles," I said.

"Ah, the national emblem of Scotland. I am not surprised that you of all people would miss a cursed weed," he said.

"Get on with your revenge, " I told him.

"There will be no violence," he said. "It is not even possible."

"Aye, then," I said. "What is the trick? Am I to die an old man takin' woolies through the mountains?"

"Ah, Alistair Angus McColley, your stubbornness has made you blind. Come, we must move on."

"You, whoever you are, you are forcin' me to go?"

"There is no force involved," he said. "Nothing done here is by human force or power." He grinned a wondrous smile and his eyes twinkled with a pure light that drained all my energy. Suddenly I could see that everythin' was too pure, too perfect.

"This isn't Scotland, is it?" I said.

"Alistair, this isn't even earth."

"Saints alive," I said. "Then I have passed on!"

"Yah, but passed over is better to say. You arrived on this shore yesterday."

"Then you really are the Big Swede," I said. "The very man felled by a blow from me shovel. Then this is hell. It is far better than I imagined."

"Shh," he warned me. "We do not speak of the other place. It is a defilement. Think, Alistair, of the letters from Reba, the Bible she sent you, the words read patiently by the nurse's aide."

Pages of my mind turned like an old photo album. The cherished letters from Reba, my only visitation except those who came askin' about gold. Gold? My precious buried treasure was worthless to me now.

"You called on the name of our Lord Jesus Christ with your dying breath, do you remember?"

"Aye," I said. "I saw darkness descending as a cloud. It pulled somethin' within me, but the words o' Reba's letters illuminated the dark and I did as she asked, I cried out to the God she served."

"That was your passage to glory, Alistair. Your Isabel brought me the news."

"Isabel, my wife?"

"Yah. And your daughters. And Sarah and Martha and a granddaughter that awaits her naming." His face glowed like that of a cherub.

"Then this be heaven," I said, feelin' like a common thief trespassin' upon the King's land.

"It is the Borderlands. True heaven lies ahead."

"But it cannot get any more glorious than this."

"This is a shadow," said the Big Swede. "It becomes far more glorious with each step toward the Highlands."

The idea gave me shudders. "I cannot take greater glory," I said. "I will stay here." I folded my arms and buried me chin in me chest.

The Big Swede shrugged. "Yah, some do. I did for a spell. But you have a job to do, Alistair. A flock to shepherd and a treasure to unearth. All will change with each crossing of The River."

"River?" I said. "I need to ford a river with a flock?"

"Yah. Three times. The first time is but a trickle, ankle-deep on most, to your knees, perhaps."

The truth was slowly settling in on me, yet I was still confused. "Karl," I said, "I cannot go further. I am a murderer. I fear this place. I do not deserve to be here."

He laughed again as if I was most amusin'. "Deserve?" he said. "It is a word you will strike from your vocabulary after you cross The River."

"No, I will stay here. There is plenty o' food. If I get cold, I will go to the geyser o' fire."

"Geyser of fire? Oh, Alistair, that is not a geyser. That is a Guardian of the Borderlands. A warrior angel. Your eyes are still too dim to see its face."

I approached an angel? I was most uncomfortable. "Is there another place?" I asked. "Somethin' less than this?"

"This is the least," he said.

"Then I will stay here," I said.

"Oh, Alistair, you've brought so much of your earthly stubbornness with you. We must move on to the Highlands."

"I have too great a burden. I could not possibly carry it to higher elevations."

"There is no burden," he said.

"Ha," I said. "I should say there is. My killin' of you. My treatment of Isabel, and everyone else for that matter."

"There you go, speaking of worth again."

"I want to talk about the day I killed you," I said.

"Talk about it? But, Alistair, I do not recall it at all."

Deep suspicion tugged at me 'art. "Ye do not remember your own dyin'?" I wondered if I was truly in the Misty Beyond.

"I'm sorry," he said. "It all washed away in The River."

I folded me arms firmer 'gainst me chest. "Well, I ain't takin' a step," I said. "Till we talk about it. How do I know you are who you say you are when ye can't recall your own dyin'?"

He looked down thoughtfully. "OK," he said. "It will wash away when we cross The River. Talk about it if you wish."

"Aye, good," I said. "Confession is good for the soul."

I proceeded to tell Karl Hannson the story of his death.

"It happened in 1966," I said. "A dry year. You had a flowin' spring on a hill that trickled down to our property. I had me grandson, Warren, irrigatin' a garden from that trickle. Ye remember now, don'tcha?"

"No, I don't recall a thing," he said.

"One hot summer day the flow stopped. I climbed the hill and found ye dikin' the stream, divertin' the flow onto your property. We argued. Ye said it was your water and I said it was mine. I grabbed the shovel from ye. Ye raised a big fist to hit me and I struck first. Ye fell across the dike and lay there like a giant, dammin' the small stream into a pond. I knew ye was dead. I looked down the hill to me house and saw the bedroom curtains parted and the little laddie, Warren, standin' there wi' terror on 'is face. Now ye recall, don'tcha, man?"

"No, no, not yet," he said.

"I marched to me house, the shovel still in me hand. I grabbed the laddie. 'Look here,' I said, 'he swung first. Ye have to tell everyone the Big Swede swung first,' and I left 'im there holdin' the blood-stained shovel."

"Well, did I swing first?" Karl asked.

"Aye, I thought so, but don't ye remember now?"

"I will tell you what I remember," Karl Hannson said. "I arrived near here in a grassy meadow. I was certain it was Sweden. It felt so very much like home. I could hear the prayers my blessed mother had taught me as I sat on her lap as a child. But I was filled with anger. I was sure it was I who had committed murder."

"You?" I said. "But how could ye think it was you?"

"Ah, here, Alistair, one learns that anger in the heart and murder upon the hands is one in the same."

"Aye, well, me murders are many then, for I lived a life of rage."

"Let us go to The River," Karl said. "You have a flock to shepherd and a treasure to unearth."

"Treasure," I said, spitting the words from me mouth. "I want nothin' o' treasure. I labored all me life for somethin' that means nothin' to me now. And how am I to dig it up? I buried it in Duncan's well."

"This is different treasure," he said. "Now come, we have a long journey ahead of us."

He began walkin' and I had to run to catch up. I did not want to go on, but I did not want to be left behind. "What am I to do in this place?" I asked.

"Shepherd the little ones," he said, and a small flock of lambs appeared before us. They were as soft and white as balls o' cotton.

"That is all?" I asked. "Just herd this little flock?"

"The little flock is only the beginning, Alistair. You have arrived like I, a babe brought in on the prayer wings of others. You have much to learn."

"When I left me home as a lad, I left all religion," I said.

"That is OK," he said. "We do not study religion here."

"What, no religion?"

"No. We study His Story."

"History?"

"Yah. His Story. In the meadows, in the mountains, in great halls of learning. Everywhere you go, you will learn and be taught His Story."

I fell in behind the lambs, but they did not move forward. They stood in a bunch and looked at me with curious eyes.

Karl watched me with a kind smile. His deep voice was filled with compassion as he spoke. "Alistair," he said, "you must lead them. You must talk to them. Your sheep know your voice and will follow you."

Ridiculous, I thought.

"No, it isn't. Speak to them."

"What do I say?"

"Say, 'Come, lambs.'"

"Come, lambs," I said, and to my amazement, they bounced with joy and followed me as I walked. Leadin' the sheep suddenly made me aware of me family. The family I had left behind. "Karl, what about those still livin'? What o' me sons, and their children, and their loved ones?"

"We know little of that life," Karl said. "For the most part, it is kept from us."

"Surely ye know somethin'?"

"Usually we look for news ourselves from new arrivals like yourself. But, of course, your situation was unusual."

"Ye must know about Duncan and Roland, and Warren, and Dickie, and Donald and Clara? Tell me about them," I pleaded.

"It is better that you wait until you have crossed The River," he said.

"No," I said and I stopped abruptly. The lambs milled about me, blattin' with fear and confusion. "I will not go a step further until you tell me."

Karl's gaze was firm but sympathetic. "All knowledge is easier once you have been washed in The River," he said.

"I must know," I said.

"Why? Can you go back? Can you do somethin' about it now?"

"There must be somethin' I can do," I said.

"Yah. You can move on with me and unearth your treasure. That is how you can help those you left behind."

"No. Not a step further. What o' me sons? What o' Roland and Duncan?"

A deep sadness covered the broad face of Karl Hannson. "They made their decisions," he said. "There will be a separation."

"Me boys are dead?"

"They are gone, Alistair."

I was overcome by a terrible grief that dropped me to me knees. I hated who I was and the life I had lived. "I cannot stay here," I said. "I would be far more comfortable in hell."

"Do not say that," Karl said firmly, and he lifted me to my feet. "We must move on."

"Why? Why should I?" I cried.

"For the sake of Warren, Dick, Donald, and Clara," he said.

I followed Karl Hannson heartlessly, failin' to notice the land grew in beauty with each of my tortured steps. "I was a curse upon me whole family," I sobbed. "I hated religion for keepin' me parents poor, and look what has come o' it."

"Forgive yourself," Karl said.

"No, never," I said.

"Do you truly hate your own life?" he asked.

"Aye, with all me heart."

"Then you are progressing well," he said.

We marched beneath a sunless sky for what could have been hours, or only minutes, I had no way of knowin', until we came to The River. It flowed softly like a ribbon of molten pearl. I could barely see to the other side, but the land there was obviously more beautiful still. The River seemed to bid me to enter.

"You can unearth the treasure now," Karl said.

"Where is it?" I asked.

He reached into the tall grass and brought out a shovel. Its handle was carved oak and the spade silver. "Dig anywhere," he said. "And it will be there."

I stepped back and plunged the spade into the rich, dark soil. Good earth. Or, good heaven, I should say. I struck somethin' solid. "I think I have found it," I said. But as I scooped the dirt out I did not see a treasure box, but a tangle o' thick black roots. The more I dug, the more o' the roots I uncovered. "There is no treasure," I said, starin' down at what looked like a den of snakes.

"Yah, there is treasure," Karl answered. "Use the blade of the shovel against the roots."

I swung the shovel as if it were an ax, bringin' it down time and time again, like a cattleman breakin' ice on a frozen pond. The roots pulsed and writhed in pain. They lashed at me like tentacles, until finally, I cut through the main stem, then the smaller roots relaxed and loosened their fisted grips to display a large metal box. Painted beautifully on its lid was the face of a smilin' woman and the words Mother's Love Baking Powder inscribed in golden script. For a brief second, me mind flashed to Duncan's well and a dark, distant world of sickness, greed, and selfishness.

Karl lifted the box to the surface. "Open it," he said.

I bent over the treasure chest and usin' me knees to hold it, I pried at the lid with me fingertips. I could feel a mighty power within the box, and I feared it would explode in me face. "It's gonna blow," I said.

Karl smiled. "Let it blow," he said.

I pulled the lid off, and an explosion of golden light cascaded into the air, followed by flutterings of a thousand wings as a spray o' butterflies took flight. They were every color o' the rainbow. Some were as big as me hands, some as small as dimes. They erupted into the sky, movin' as a single stream o' beauty with music radiatin' from their wings.

"What are they?" I asked.

"The prayers of godly women," Karl said.

"Where are they goin'?" I asked.

"To where they were always intended. To the hearts of the men the women love."

I gave him a stupefied look. "But they were bound-up by those thick roots," I said. "What were they?"

"The bitterness of sin," he said.

"The bitterness o' me own sin," I said.

"Yah, you are learning," Karl said, and he began movin' to the water. "I must go now," he called back to me. "Follow at your own pace."

I gazed across the pearly stream. The trees were taller and richer on the distant bank, and a glow emanated from the horizon. "Is the sun finally risin'?" I asked.

"We have no need of a sun," he said.

"But the glow—"

"It is the light that shines from the music of praise," he said. He was only ankle-deep in The River, but his whole body glistened as if it were wet.

"I can't enter The River," I yelled to him. "I am too tainted. I would only pollute it."

"You underestimate The River," he called back.

"No. No, I don't," I said.

"Then you overestimate your sin," he answered.

I moved to the stream's edge. The lambs crowded about me as if urgin' me in. I touched The River with one bare foot, and no words can describe the very power o' purity that washed through me. I felt confusion, guilt, and fear drainin' away by a mere sprinklin' o' water. Above me I caught the faint glimmer o' butterfly wings and the soft melody of their harmonious song. I thought o' Reba and her letters.

Karl Hannson stood halfway across the sparklin'
River, his face glowin' golden and his arms raised in a
wave. "Come on in," he shouted. "The water's fine."

". . . And such were the resolute, stoic men who
pioneered the arid northern plains. Men who
embarked on dangerous pilgrimages from one world to
another, to a land vastly distant and vastly different.
They endured incredible hardships. They were proud,
capable men. Men of grit, gumption, and guts. Alistair
Angus McColley was one of them. He was a man of
obvious faults, not a saint, but a sinner, and in that he
was no more and no less than we."

The banquet room was silent for a long moment, then
a soft, respectful applause trickled through the audience. The overhead lights came on and my husband,
Donald McColley, stepped from behind the podium. I
was standing, and the others, taking my stance as a cue,
rose to give Donald an ovation. He blushed, his bald
head reddening like a Christmas light.

I felt awakened, emerging from a catlike dream that
had sat curled in my lap all evening. I had to capture it
by the tail to keep it from escaping. The ghostly scenery
of hell and the colors of heaven swirled in my mind amid
the whispered secrets from the cellars of souls. I knew
where the body of Duncan McColley lay, I knew of
buried treasure, the fate of both Alistair and the Big
Swede, the covered fears of the flesh and blood around
me, and yet, all that I knew was slowly ebbing away.
Reality was exerting its return.

Donald took my arm as he came by. "How did I do?" he asked.

"You were terrific," I said, though I had heard only the last words of his speech.

The elderly guests came bearing congratulations. "I almost thought I heard old Alistair himself," I heard one say.

Warren approached and offered Donald his hand. "First-rate presentation," he said.

Donald looked at him suspiciously.

"I mean it," Warren said. "You have the soul of a poet. I wouldn't mind reading some of your work some time."

"Really?" Donald asked.

"Really." Then he turned to me. "Send me books," he said. I was slow in responding and could feel the probing of his trained, analytical mind. "Reba, are you OK?" he asked.

I became convincingly superficial. "I'm fine," I said. "It was so wonderful to have you here."

"I'm serious about the books," he said.

"You know I will send them," I laughed. "After all, I am Reba-the-Letter-Writer."

"Yes," he said. "You are."

"Why don't you come see us?" I asked. "You could pick up the books yourself."

"I could stop on my way back," he said. "Great Falls is not so far out of my way."

"I will have the books ready. When should we expect you?"

"Three or four days. There are some things I want to do here in Yellow Rock," he said.

"Time to close windows?" I asked.

"No," he said. "A time to open them."

Dick and Marci approached. Dick put his arm around Warren's shoulders. It was the first real physical contact between the two I had seen all evening. Marci gave me a hug. "Donald was great," she said. "He honored Grandpa Alistair without excusing his actions. It was amazing."

"You can count on me to be among the amazed," I said.

She whispered in my ear, "Listen, what I said about divorce? Forget it, OK"?

"It's forgotten," I said.

Dick McColley stood strong and sober. "Tell Donald I said he was a top hand with words," he said.

"Tell him yourself," I challenged.

"You be my lips," he said. "My thoughts and my mouth don't always work together."

"Send him something," I said impulsively. "An old bit or spur, something he can write a poem about."

"He'd want somethin' like that?" Dick asked.

"He would love it. Especially from you."

"I can do that," he said. "I even have a good story that I could tell him. It would make a great poem."

"I'm sure it's a very good story," I said, and felt again the breaking of his ribs.

"Well, we should be goin'," Dick said. "Marci wants to be in church tomorrow. Won't hurt me to go either,

I suppose." Marci's eyes lit up with surprise. A rock had rolled from the tomb, exposing her husband's heart. She flashed me a neon smile.

Dick's arm was still around Warren, who seemed covered by the embrace. He melted into it.

"Come visit us, big brother," Dick said.

"Uh, to Plentywood?" Warren asked.

"Come on up. It's cold and barren, but it's home. We can nail an old backboard up on the barn, and I'll let you take the fiftieth shot."

Warren smiled. "I can be there tomorrow," he said. I saw a lone figure on a shadowed court. I heard the sweet sound of a ball passing through a rimless net.

Marci kissed me on the cheek. "Good-bye, Reba," she said. "We will need to talk about tonight sometime."

"We must," I said. And I meant it.

"Keep praying for us," she whispered.

"Don't underestimate your own prayers," I said.

The three of them left together.

An anxious museum official approached me. "Mrs. McColley," he said. "Your husband gave a great speech, but I'm sorry, it's not on tape. Something went wrong. The tape is blank."

"That's OK," I told him. "Maybe it is more special this way."

I eased my way past people and collected Donald's and my coats. On the way back, I bumped into Pete and Clara. Clara's face was stern, but the corners of her eyes were wet with tears.

"Tell Donald he did real well," she said.

"I'm sure he would like to hear it from you," I said.

She shook her head. She wasn't ready for that much risk. I knew she might not approve, but I gave her a hug. "Don't worry," I told her. "Everything is going to work out fine." A slight tremble of fear passed through her tight, hard body.

"I guess I don't know my brother," she said.

I looked at her curiously. Her body was slowly yielding to my embrace.

"I thought I did," she said. "Until tonight."

"And we don't know either of you as well as we should," I said. I released her hand and she pulled back to Pete who stood quietly, his black hat in his hands.

"Donald done good," he said. My eyes looked on his. Of all the people in the room, I suspected Pete had seen and heard more than anyone.

"You are both a treasure," I said. "A treasure that needs to come to light."

Pete's eyes were firm. "Nothin' should stay in the dark," he said.

Our eyes clashed lightly. I wanted more. He was not to give it. He put a protective arm around Clara. "I need to be gettin' my wife home," he said. I suspected he had somethin' to confess.

"Seek ye first the Kingdom," Clara blurted. My mouth dropped with pleasant surprise. She smiled and dabbed at her eyes with the cuff of her blouse. "Somethin' my mother always said," she explained. She looked girlish and vulnerable; Pete was boyish and possessive. They turned and left, clinging to one another so tightly it was hard to see where one ended and the other began.

I rejoined Donald. He looked tired and eager to be rescued from the few storytellers that remained.

"The tape recorder didn't work," I told him.

"That's OK," he said.

"It's OK?"

"Yeah. I wish the kids could hear it, but—"

"But you can tell them yourself?"

"Yeah."

"Clara and Pete liked your speech," I said.

"They did. Well, where are they?"

"They just left."

"We should catch them," he said. "Invite them up for Thanksgiving or something."

"Donald, Thanksgiving is eight months away."

"Well, Easter, then. That's soon, isn't it?"

"It's a wonderful idea," I said. "But don't you think they will be busy calving?"

His forehead wrinkled and his eyebrows knitted together. This was a sign of being in deep thought. "Well, we could visit them," he said.

I remembered Duncan. I remembered Pete knowing. "I'm sure we will all be getting together soon," I said. "But it wouldn't hurt to bring them a turkey for Easter."

"Let's see if we can find them," Donald said. He was a man on a mission, a man who wanted to do something before he talked himself out of it.

We stepped out into the cool Montana night. A million stars seemed to shine overhead as the bundled elderly walked with labored steps to their vehicles. They moved like shadows in a dark world. We looked about. There was no sign of Pete and Clara.

Donald, who was always in a hurry to go everywhere, stopped. "Look up," he said. "Look at those stars."

We turned our faces toward the heavens. I put my gloved hand in his.

"It's not that our world is so small," he said. "It's that the universe is so great."

I squeezed his hand. "Sounds like you have another poem in you," I said.

Donald laughed. It was the first time I had heard him laugh in years. "Undammed," he said. "I feel undammed."

The river was flowing. I could feel the pull and tug of its power.

And he showed me a pure river of water of life, clear as crystal, proceeding from the throne of God and of the Lamb. In the middle of its street, and on either side of the river, was the tree of life, which bore twelve fruits, each tree yielding its fruit every month. The leaves of the tree were for the healing of the nations. And there shall be no more curse, but the throne of God and of the Lamb shall be in it, and His servants shall serve Him.

Revelation 22:1-3

ABOUT THE AUTHOR

John L. Moore is an award-winning writer whose articles and short stories have been published in *The New York Times Magazine*, *Reader's Digest* and many other publications. He received the Critic's Choice for Fiction Award from *Christianity Today* for his first novel, *The Breaking of Ezra Riley*, which Thomas Nelson plans to release again in Spring, 1994.

John lives with his wife, Debra, and their two children on a ranch near Miles City, Montana.